The moment...

I can hear Battle breathing—is it louder than usual? Faster? Or is that mine I hear?

I swallow a couple of times. I really should have gotten myself something to drink, too.

"I can't feel any hair," I announce, and step away.

I remember when I first saw Battle and thought of her as Beautiful Hair Girl. She's still beautiful, of course. But now, with her head shaved, she looks much more vulnerable. Smaller. It makes me want to protect her. I don't know from what.

"Ooh yuck, I have little tiny hairs all down my shirt," Battle says rapidly, in a higher voice than usual. She uses both hands to pinch her shirt at the shoulders, then shakes it in an attempt to dislodge the hairs.

"That's not gonna work, you'll have to take a shower," I say automatically. Then an incredibly vivid picture of Battle in the shower forms itself in my brain. Special effects, cue the Nicola Lancaster Special Neon Blush. Again? Yep, again.

OTHER BOOKS YOU MAY ENJOY

Sara Ryan

Empress of the World

EXPANDED EDITION

Introduction by David Levithan

speak
An Imprint of Penguin Group (USA) Inc.

Thanks:
Mom and Dad, all the friends I conned into reading drafts
(you know who you are), UWG, STEW, Sharyn, David,
and especially Steve.

SPEAK
Published by the Penguin Group
Penguin Group (USA) Inc., 345 Hudson Street, New York, New York 10014, U.S.A.
Penguin Group (Canada), 90 Eglinton Avenue East, Suite 700, Toronto, Ontario, Canada M4P 2Y3
(a division of Pearson Penguin Canada Inc.)
Penguin Books Ltd, 80 Strand, London WC2R 0RL, England
Penguin Ireland, 25 St Stephen's Green, Dublin 2, Ireland (a division of Penguin Books Ltd)
Penguin Group (Australia), 250 Camberwell Road, Camberwell, Victoria 3124, Australia
(a division of Pearson Australia Group Pty Ltd)
Penguin Books India Pvt Ltd, 11 Community Centre, Panchsheel Park, New Delhi – 110 017, India
Penguin Group (NZ), 67 Apollo Drive, Rosedale, Auckland 0632, New Zealand
(a division of Pearson New Zealand Ltd)
Penguin Books (South Africa) (Pty) Ltd, 24 Sturdee Avenue, Rosebank, Johannesburg 2196, South Africa

Registered Offices: Penguin Books Ltd, 80 Strand, London WC2R 0RL, England

First published in the United States of America by Viking,
a division of Penguin Putnam Books for Young Readers, 2001
First published by Speak, an imprint of Penguin Group (USA) Inc., 2003
This Speak edition published 2012

15 17 19 20 18 16 14

"Me and Edith Head" originally appeared in *Cicada* magazine, Vol. 4, No. 1, 2002,
and was subsequently published by Cold Water Press, 2003.
Four short quotes from *How to Dress for Success* by Edith Head and Joe Hyams,
which appear in "Me and Edith Head," quotes copyright © 1967 by Edith Head with Joe Hyams,
used with permission of Sterling Lord Literistic, Inc.
"Click" was originally published by Cold Water Press, 2007.
"Comparative Anatomy" appears here for the first time in any form.

THE LIBRARY OF CONGRESS HAS CATALOGED THE VIKING EDITION AS FOLLOWS:
Ryan, Sara.
Empress of the world / Sara Ryan.
p. cm.
Summary: While attending a summer institute, fifteen-year-old Nic meets another girl named Battle,
falls in love with her, and finds the relationship to be difficult and confusing.
ISBN 0-670-89688-8 (hc)
[1. Lesbians—Fiction. 2. Homosexuality—Fiction. 3. Bisexuality—Fiction. 4. Schools—Fiction.]
I. Title. PZ7.R957 Em 2001 [Fic]—dc21 00-052758

Speak ISBN 978-0-14-250059-0

Printed in the United States of America

for Victoria, Susan,
and Harry

INTRODUCTION

Dear Archaeologists of the Future,

In your hand you have a copy of Sara Ryan's lovely novel *Empress of the World*. It is not, as the title may lead you to believe, the story of a woman who takes over Earth. The world in this novel is much smaller than that. More intimate. More illuminating.

If you are curious about what it was like to be a teenager at the start of the twenty-first century, I think there are few better places to start than this novel. You may have also excavated advertisement images from this time—Abercrombie boys and CK girls who seem as vapid as they are attractive. You may even find TV shows where the teenagers come across as overarticulate mini-adults, or movies where they are portrayed as sex-crazed idiots, often slain by serial killers in masks. Please do not look at those representations. Please look at novels like this instead.

The author of this book realizes something very important: Teenagers are smart. They sometimes do stupid things, out of either ignorance or sheer stupidity, but by and large they are thoughtful human beings, trying to piece together both their own worlds and the world at large. Sometimes adults help. Sometimes they don't. Sometimes truths are discovered easily. Sometimes they are only discovered through profound heartbreak, disappointment, and pain.

When this book was first published, much was made of the fact that it involves two girls who fall in love with each other. In the history of literature, especially literature for teenagers, such entanglements often led to misery, despondency, and sometimes death. (There were, mercifully, some exceptions to the rule—see Ryan's tip of the hat to *Weetzie Bat*, and if you don't know what she's talking about, excavate copies of Francesca Lia Block's books.) As the twenty-first century dawned, a sea change occurred, and this novel was one at the vanguard of showing a much more realistic picture of what it's like to be a lesbian, bisexual, and/or questioning teenager. Ryan shows that love is love, and that while same-sex love may look different to some from the outside, from the inside you can see the truth, which is that you never fall in love with a gender, but a person.

I am trusting that by the time you read this, such truths will be commonplace. Even in the past decade, the world has changed so much, and has proven to be full of many more Katrinas and Isaacs than there are Andys and Bens. (You'll know what I mean after you read the book.) This is not a book about coming out so much as it is a book about coming into love. Which I imagine is still a very delicate, fearful, wonderful, agonizing, remarkable thing.

So piece together these pages, and you'll see what it's

like to escape your high school for a summer, to find your-self confronted by possibilities, and then to grow up as you decide which of the possibilities are truly yours, and what you must do to make them reality. This is what is was like for us, when we were not quite old, but no longer that young. The inside of our hearts is captured herein.

Sincerely,
David Levithan
Author of the Past, Asked to Introduce This Novel in 2012

P.S. Pay close attention to page 52. If the phrase "He must be going completely bugfuck, don't you think?" no longer exists, please bring it back.

O Fortuna
velut luna
statu variabilis,
semper crescis
aut decrescis . . .

O Fortune, you are changeable like the moon, ever waxing
and waning . . .

–from "Fortuna Imperatrix Mundi"
(Fortune, Empress of the World),
Carmina Burana, Cantiones Profanae

Part One

June 14, 4 p.m.,
Prucher Hall Auditorium

I am sitting cross-legged on an uncomfortable seat, waiting for a speech to start. It has been approximately forty-five minutes since Mom and Dad left me here. I am going to be here for the whole summer, and I do not know a single person.

I open my big new journal. So far all it has is a title page which says "Field Notes" in block letters. I turn to the first blank page and write:

hypothesis: taking an actual class in archaeology will serve to confirm nicola lancaster in her lifelong dream of becoming an archaeologist.

I scratch out "lifelong dream," because it doesn't sound scientific enough, and write "proposed vocation," but that sounds pompous, so I write "lifelong dream" again, and then above it, in larger letters, "ignore: this is dumb." Then I write: "speech notes" just in case I actually take any.

A large pink bald man in a navy blue suit that's slightly too small for him walks up to the podium in the middle of the stage. He taps the microphone a couple of times until he gets the proper loud staticky clicking sound.

"Greetings, everyone. I'm so pleased to welcome you all to the Siegel Institute Summer Program for Gifted Youth. You are exceptionally talented, and we at the institute are privileged to serve as guides for this stage of your educational explorations."

if you bottled his voice, you would never have to buy cooking oil again.

I look around.

who else is being forced to listen?
scary-looking kids in the front. guys with bad hair, button-down shirts, and ties. girls in perfect pastel floral-print dresses. one redheaded guy wearing a three-piece suit. mostly white, some asians, a few black kids. as usual, each ethnic group member is only sitting with other people from the same ethnic group. four disgusted-looking girls sitting together, dressed in all black with dyed black hair: the goth ethnic group?

Two seats over on the right is a tall, solid girl with gray-blue eyes and a lot of curly red hair. She is wearing a green velvet dress and black sandals, and is carefully painting her toenails the same shade of green as the dress. Her fingernails are purple. I start to sketch her. I want to see if I can get her hair and her look of total concentration.

I get her expression but screw up her hair, then ruin her expression in the process of trying to fix her hair.

On my left are a boy and another girl. The boy has wavy, longish, dark brown hair, caterpillaresque eyebrows, octagonal glasses, and I don't know what his eyes look like; they're closed. He won't notice me drawing because he's asleep. Deeply asleep—I see drool glistening at one corner of his mouth.

I draw his closed eyes and his open mouth. I have a hard time with the drool. It ends up looking more prominent than it actually is.

I look back up on stage. "It is necessary to understand that giftedness *qua* giftedness, that is to say giftedness *as* giftedness, is not sufficient armor with which to attack the modern world."

you don't attack with armor. armor is a defense.

I sketch Large Pink Bald Man: an egg with arms and legs, and a smaller egg on top for the head. The resemblance to Humpty Dumpty is uncanny, so I draw a wall, then a second sketch—of his great fall. *Splat.*

The girl on my left has the most beautiful hair I have ever seen. It's blonde and very long, thick, simple, and heavy. All the blonde girls I know do so much crap to their hair. They curl, spray, and gel it into submission. Actually, that's not true; there are the hippie girls who part it in the middle and braid it, but they're the exception. This girl's hair doesn't look like that. You'd think that with the heat, she'd put it up, but it's just hanging down her back. And it's blonde, all right, but not platinum blonde, and not that really yellowy blonde, either. Honey is the closest color, but it would have to be different kinds of honey that are different shades, like alfalfa and clover, and maybe some spices too, like ginger and cumin. Of course, this doesn't really matter, because all I have is a pencil and I doubt I could get her hair right if I had the world's biggest box of crayons. I couldn't get her eyes right, either. They're so green. They look like they would glow in the dark.

I realize I haven't drawn anything yet. I quickly sketch the shape of her head and start doing her hair. The nose will be hard; I always mess up noses. Maybe I should do the mouth first. She has narrow lips.

For a while I forget where I am. I'm trying to be like Dad, to look at her the way he looks at things when he draws. He says he breaks objects up into forms: like he doesn't see a head, he sees an oval.

But I just keep seeing this girl.

She has her index finger in her mouth. I can't quite tell, but it looks like she's peeling off the skin around her cuticle with her teeth.

I didn't think anyone else did that.

I know I'm drawing too quickly and sloppily now, but I want to have evidence that someone else damages herself in the same small subtle way. She takes her finger out of her mouth too fast for me to capture it on paper, but when she does, I see a spot of blood. Beautiful Hair Girl has messed-up fingers like mine.

Just as I'm thinking this, she looks over at me with those glow-in-the-dark green eyes. I feel myself start to blush. Then she smiles. After a moment, I smile back.

"One of the most important parts of your experience at the Siegel Institute will be making friends with your peers, and you will have many opportunities to do so. But I must caution you strongly that initiating, uh, romantic connections is not an appropriate use of your time here. You are all mature young people and I have every confidence that you understand the issues involved." LPBM clears his throat several times and takes a sip of water.

"Jesus, somebody must have gotten pregnant last year," the Redhead mutters.

LPBM starts talking about all the other things we are supposedly mature enough not to do: drink, take drugs, steal, cheat, destroy university property. Then he says, "If you find yourself dealing with any difficult issues, I encourage you to bring them to your Residence Advisor. They are all trained counselors and they are here to help you."

I take a chance and whisper, "She got pregnant and then killed herself." I hear a snort of suppressed laughter from the Redhead.

When Large Pink Bald Man finally shuts up, people applaud in relief. The applause wakes up Drooling Boy, and the Redhead pokes me in the arm and says, "Hey! You were drawing the whole time! Can I see?"

I'm frozen. It's like she asked me to take my clothes off. But I can't figure out how to say no, so I hand her the notebook. Almost immediately, confirming my worst fears, she starts laughing.

"You are so totally right about his voice! That's hilarious!" she says, pointing to my cooking oil comment.

I'm so relieved that I can't think of anything to say, so I just smile. "These are great!" she continues. Then she addresses Formerly Drooling Boy. "Hey, *you!*"

He has already gotten up to leave the auditorium. He's wiping off his mouth, looking embarrassed. She beckons. "Come over here, and get the girl next to you, too!"

The Redhead says, "Oh, I'm totally sorry, I didn't even

ask if it was okay—but you guys, look, she's an artist! She drew all three of us during that heinous speech! Isn't it cool?" She passes my notebook to Formerly Drooling Boy.

"Was I that bad?" he asks. I shrug. He passes the notebook to Beautiful Hair Girl, and I feel suddenly even more tense. She studies it intently for a minute or two. "Those are excellent. My name is Battle." She restores my notebook to me, and I clutch it to my chest like a stuffed animal.

"I'm Nicola, but most people call me Nic," I say.

Battle looks at me with a strange expression, as though what I've just said is far more shocking than I think it is. I know I have a bizarre name, but hers is worse.

The Redhead says, "I'm Katrina—and please tell me you don't hate me because I got all excited about your art! I'm always doing things like that, all the time. Who are you?" She turns to Formerly Drooling Boy.

"Uh, Isaac."

We all smile at each other, not knowing what comes next.

"Battle," Katrina says. "I've never heard that name before. Were your parents anti-hippies who named you to protest all the babies called Love and Peace and Sunshine?"

"No," Battle says. "Battle Hall is the building where my parents met. I'm named after a building; it's too weird." She grimaces.

"I'm named after a scientist," I say, surprising myself. "Scientists are almost as weird as buildings." Battle grins.

"What scientist?" asks Isaac.

"Nikola Tesla. I don't really understand anything that he did, but my parents love him."

"Oh, Tesla, right! Are they scientists?" asks Katrina.

"Mom is. Dad isn't," I say.

"We're the only ones left," Battle says, looking around. "Let's vacate."

When we get outside, Katrina says, "Hold on a second, guys," and digs in the huge black bag she's carrying. After a minute or two, she triumphantly holds up a pack of American Spirits. "Now I just need to find the lighter. . . ." She says this with a cigarette already in her mouth.

"Hey, give me one of those," says Isaac. She does.

"I've led a sheltered life. You guys both smoke?" I ask.

Katrina says, "I do." She reaches over and takes the cigarette out of Isaac's mouth. "He doesn't. You want the end with the filter on it closer to your mouth." She sticks the cigarette behind her ear.

"I just did that to see if you'd notice," mumbles Isaac. He's blushing a little. "I don't feel like a cigarette right now, anyway."

"How long have you been smoking?" I ask Katrina.

"Too long," she says. "I'm going to quit soon. I promised myself. It's just that things are so stressful right now."

She inhales deeply. She sounds very Eastern. I wonder if she's from New York.

"Smoking is foul. I'm going to get dinner," says Battle, holding her nose. She starts walking towards the cafeteria, and after a moment, the rest of us follow her.

"Come on, you all should ask for kosher," says Isaac as we're standing in line for some as yet unidentifiable but reddish and vaguely pasta-like substance.

"Why?" asks Katrina.

"Well, I was here last year, and the deal is that if you want kosher, they have to make it for you specially, and that means it has a fighting chance of being decent. Plus it pisses them off, but they can't say anything 'cause it would be anti-Semitism."

It sounds good to me, but Katrina shakes her head. "I think it's far more important to continue my campaign to have ranch dressing recognized as a food group."

"Ranch dressing is grotesque," I say.

"Ranch dressing is a food group," Katrina counters.

"I'm with her. Ranch dressing rocks," an unfamiliar voice says from behind Katrina. It belongs to a gangly Asian guy with long hair pulled back in a ponytail, an army jacket, baggy jeans shorts, white socks, and what I can only think of as concert shoes—black patent leather, formal looking, like what we have to wear for orchestra concerts at school.

11

"Thank you, citizen, for that unsolicited testimonial. I'm Katrina, and you are?"

"Kevin."

We all tell him our names, and he smiles in a slow sleepy way. I wonder whether he's on drugs or just chronically mellow.

"What are you in for?" Battle asks him.

Kevin looks confused.

"I think she means what class are you taking," I translate.

"Oh—right, like jail. That's funny," he says, without laughing. Then, after a few moments of silence, he adds, "Uh, music. Theory."

I say, "My viola teacher wanted me to go to some of those classes because I can't take lessons this summer, but I don't actually know what music theory even is. What is it?"

Kevin blinks a couple of times. It's like we're in a chat room and he's got a really slow connection. Finally he says, "It's the underlying structures that make composition possible." After a few more seconds, he adds, vaguely, "Modes."

I have studied viola for over five years and I have no idea what he's talking about. Maybe he's making it up.

"So music theory is something *you* want to do," says Battle. "As opposed to what your parents want."

Kevin nods, and moves next to me and Battle in line.

"You, too?" asks Isaac.

Battle nods. "World History, joy oh rapture."

"I took that last year; it was okay," says Isaac. "Taking what your parents want is such a waste. But when it's either that or having to spend the summer with them—" Isaac starts, and Katrina finishes, "You take what you can get."

I laugh along with everyone else, but it makes me feel a little strange. Am I the only person here who likes her parents?

Isaac asks for a kosher meal, and then looks horrified when he's handed an unidentifiable khaki mass that looks even less appetizing than the red mass the rest of us are waiting for. "Stuffed cabbage," says the guy behind the counter. "We had so much demand last year they decided to have some kosher stuff premade for each meal."

"Shit," says Isaac.

"No, cabbage!" says Katrina cheerily. Then she asks the guy, "Can I get a salad and, like, seven extra things of ranch dressing?" He lets her.

"That is so unbelievably gross," I say. Katrina just laughs, and arranges the dressing packets on her tray into the shape of a K.

"So what are you, a vegetarian?" the guy asks me.

"What do I get if I am?" I ask.

"Grilled cheese sandwich. Green beans," he answers.

"Yeah!" I say. That's my all-time favorite lunch, except

for the green beans. "You'll have to wait a few minutes," he says. The magic words.

"Fine," I say, grinning. Kevin decides to be a vegetarian, too.

Katrina, Battle, and I sit together in a row on one side of the table, which makes both Isaac and Kevin look slightly disappointed. Isaac obviously wanted to sit with Katrina—but did Kevin want to sit with me, or Battle?

They sit across from us and spread out in a boylike way, taking up the maximum possible amount of space.

"You were here last year, too," Isaac says suddenly to Battle. She nods.

"What's it like?" I ask.

"Well, I'm back," says Battle.

Isaac shrugs. "It's better than staying home."

"You got that right." Battle takes a contemplative sip of iced tea, makes a face, and dumps several packets of sugar into her glass. Then she says, "But I think this year will be different."

"Different how?" asks Isaac.

Battle shakes her head. "I don't know. Just different."

I wonder if Battle made friends here last year. And if they came back. But if they had, wouldn't she be sitting with them instead?

"Well, of course it will be different! You obviously didn't fall into such fabulous company last year. I personally guarantee that everything will be at least fifty percent more interesting this year," says Katrina, flourishing her fork like a magician, narrowly missing knocking over Kevin's soda. "And it will be even better if you all drop your classes and take Computer Science with me. It'll be great, you'll see!"

"It's better not to be in classes with friends," Battle says.

Are we that already?

My heart actually starts to beat a little bit faster.

It's not like I have *no* friends back home, but they are all associated with activities: theater friends, orchestra friends. I'm pretty short on just plain *friend* friends.

"Just because then you pay more attention," she continues. "I mean it's lame, but it helps." She takes a bite of lasagna, which is apparently what the red mass is supposed to be.

"Geek!" accuses Isaac.

"This is goddamn geek HQ, in case you hadn't noticed," Battle says. With an elegant hand gesture, she indicates the other tables full of kids, most of whom look like they always sit by themselves at their regular school.

"I have to see if I really want to be an archaeologist. That's sort of the whole point of this summer," I explain to Katrina.

"Why do you *think* you want to be one?" Katrina asks.

Spotlight on Nic. I blush and mumble, "I guess . . . I just like the idea of fitting pieces together. Figuring out how people lived. Mapping it all out."

"You don't want to find treasure?" Battle asks, sounding slightly disappointed.

I shake my head. "Just plain people from the past, how they worked, what they were like," I say.

"Then the teacher will love you," says Battle. "At least if it's the same one as last year. If it's a different one—"

"You'll decide to do something totally different with your life, and it'll all be because of this summer," Isaac says in a deep scary horror movie preview voice.

"My mom said she became a software developer because the coolest guys were in those classes in college," Katrina says.

"Your mom must have some weirdass taste in guys," says Kevin in the draggy way he seems to say everything.

"Don't even get me started," says Katrina, holding up her hands to discourage us further from getting her started. "I mean, at least my dad has, like, some personal hygiene standards! Not that he has any other kind, mind you. But Mom's last couple of boyfriends—ugh, not even."

So Katrina's parents are divorced.

"Who else's parents are divorced?" I ask. There's silence. After a little while, Katrina says to me,

"So we're the only products of broken homes, huh, Nic? We'll have to stick together."

I say quickly, "Oh, my parents aren't divorced. I mean, they almost got divorced a while ago, but they're better now. They're actually traveling this summer, which is one of the reasons I'm here. My dad's an artist and he's traveling to different summer art fairs and stuff. And Mom's coming with him even though she's a scientist." God, Nic, shut up, who cares?

"What kind of artist?" asks Isaac.

I shrug. "He draws. Teaches. He's kind of goofy."

"Aha! DNA rules all!" says Katrina. "Nic, show Kevin your notebook!"

I don't want to show Kevin my notebook. I want to go back to my room and write in it.

But again, I don't know how to say no, so I hand it over.

"See, she's an artist, too, just like her dad! Isn't that cool?" says my personal redheaded cheering section.

Kevin looks at the sketches. He looks at the one of Battle longer than the other two. I must have really screwed that one up. "Awesome," he says finally, and gives me the notebook back.

"Oh, man, you guys, don't make her all conceited—you know they were weak," says Isaac. Then he grins.

I say, "Thanks for telling the truth, Isaac." I smile at him.

"Yeah, well, someone has to." He takes a bite of his stuffed cabbage and grimaces. "It's not bad once you get used to the texture."

"What was that about telling the truth, again?" asks Katrina.

June 15, 1:30 a.m., My Room

<u>field notes:</u>
isaac:
-is from san francisco
-was here last year (took world history, remembered battle)
-is funny
-seems nice

kevin:
-is from seattle
-dresses interestingly
-is a bizarre combination of incomprehensibly smart and incomprehensibly stupid. maybe he's just stupid.

...i know much more about battle and katrina b/c the 3 of us went to k's room after dinner and were there till after 1 a.m.!

katrina

—smokes (duh)

—is from new york, but is now living in santa fe which she hates ("men with ponytails and kokopelli earrings have no reason to exist")

—her laptop is covered with stickers and writing in black marker and is named ada after ada byron lovelace who i have never heard of before but was i guess important

—has had sex online (!!) but not in real life yet ("santa fe boys bite the flaming donkey weinie")

—has a purple stuffed penguin, many green and red plastic lizards, and a giant orange beanbag that she uses instead of a desk chair

—keeps all her clothes in a huge cardboard box

battle:

—hates smoking

—is from north carolina (slight drawl)

—has two dogs named dante and beatrice that are a special kind that starts with a c but not collies

—is a minister's daughter (!!)

—has gone out with guys, but "it's always just to a movie and then to the waffle house"

—her parents "pretty much keep me chained up to

the house like the dogs" and don't let her do
anything (but she's gone out with guys??)

    things k and b have in common:
    -prettier than i am, especially battle
    -better senses of style than me
    -more confident in groups than me
this is depressing! so instead i will write down the
things we all have in common:
    -theater!!! i do lights and sets, katrina does
costumes and acts, and battle dances. "it's better
being onstage when you don't have to talk."
    -taste in books (lord of the rings, madeline
l'engle, ursula k. leguin)
    -hated elementary school
    -never go to school dances (battle says she
intended to go to one back in middle school, but
when she was within twenty feet of the building and
could already hear the horrendously bad music, she
just turned around and walked home)
    -have parents who are older than other people's
our age
    -all on our periods right now (what are the odds
against that??)

June 15, 7:30 a.m., My Room

I can barely lift my hand to hit the snooze button on my new alarm clock, but as soon as I do, I jerk fully awake, suddenly paranoid that I didn't set it right last night and I'm already late to class. You'd think that at nearly sixteen, I would know how to operate a simple device like an alarm clock, but you'd be wrong.

But it really is seven-thirty A.M., not P.M. So I launch myself out of bed, walk over to the wall by the door, and look into the mirror. My hair is fine—that's the advantage of long, straight, boring hair. But then again, it is also long, straight, and boring. And not red, despite the fact that just a few weeks ago, I spent two hours with henna, tinfoil, and towels wrapped around my head. It apparently *wants* to be brown, and whatever I do to convince it otherwise fails to signify.

I wonder what Battle and Katrina are going to wear today.

I put on a black T-shirt and, after a minute, the same black shorts as yesterday. I feel like they're not the right shape—not long enough, or loose enough—but the T-shirt is huge—it's one of Dad's that I stole—so the shorts don't matter so much. It's not quite hot enough for sandals yet, so I put on green socks and green high-tops. I can hear my semi-friend Margaret: "Nic, you're such a techie, do you even *own* a skirt?"

Tech people always wear black, because you spend the show backstage, and you don't want the audience to be able to see you. And you're not about to wear a skirt when you have to climb the ladder up to the catwalk to hang lights.

When I get down to breakfast, I see that I'm dressed almost exactly like Isaac, which is embarrassing. The only difference is that he's wearing sandals. I don't see Kevin— maybe he sleeps late.

Battle's in a sleeveless dark blue blouse, tan leggings, and brown leather boots. Katrina has a white dress with pictures of buildings and people silk-screened onto it in black—it's like she's wearing a silent movie—neon green tights, and purple combat boots. She has her hair up, clipped into several clothespins that she has spray-painted silver.

I am boring. They probably don't even want to talk to me.

"Hey, Nic! Over here!" yells Katrina.

I can't stop smiling.

Appropriately enough, the Archaeology classroom is in the basement. There are more desks than people; there are only about twenty of us in the class.

The teacher—professor, actually, which is a big deal because a lot of the other classes are taught by graduate students—is sitting on the edge of her desk with her legs crossed, holding a coffee mug from the dining hall.

Her name, which she has written on the board in large sloppy letters, is Ms. Fraser. She pushes her curly brown hair out of her eyes and says, "This is the Archaeology class. Anyone who's here expecting anything else should leave now. Don't be embarrassed, we've all gone into the wrong room at one time or another."

No one leaves. She continues. "All right. So first off, we're going to go around the room and you're each going to say your name and why you want to study archaeology."

Most people's answers are boring: "It just looked like it would be interesting." Two boys, Alex and Ben, are arrogant, too: "I wanted something challenging—I'm so far ahead of my grade level that there's really nothing for me at my regular school." "I was already studying Greek and Latin, so I thought this would make a good addition." The only funny answer comes from a girl wearing all black in the back of the room: "I want to desecrate graves." I don't think she meant it to be funny, though.

I'm last, and I tell the truth, that I've wanted to be an archaeologist since I knew what archaeology was. "And when was that?" asks Ms. Fraser.

"When I read *Come, Tell Me How You Live*—it's this book Agatha Christie wrote about going on a dig with her husband," I say.

Anne, the girl next to me, says, "I read that too!" We smile at each other.

Ms. Fraser takes a sip of coffee, then says, "All right, people, now that we all know each other so intimately, I'm going to talk at you for a while. I don't have very much time with you—this is a third as much time as I get when I'm teaching college—so I'm going to go fast." She goes on: "I'm here to tell you the truth, and I'm telling you now so you can get out while you still can and sign up for English Lit or Political Science.

"Archaeology is garbage."

She takes another sip of coffee.

"Let me say that again, in case you didn't catch it. *Archaeology is garbage.* It is, to be precise, the art of sorting through the fragments that people have left behind, and trying to draw conclusions about their lives and their cultures based on those fragments.

"Your job in this class is to learn various ways to find the garbage, and then various other ways to classify it once you've found it. You won't get a lot of hands-on in this course, and I'm sorry about that, but at the very least you'll get to visit an in-progress dig, and you may get to do more than that—I'm still working out some details. Any questions so far?"

"Yes, I have a question. I want to know how you can call the promulgation of the whole human race garbage. I think it's totally disrespectable and I'm surprised that you as a professor would indulge in such mockery."

This comes from Alex, Arrogant Boy Number One.

Ms. Fraser blinks a couple of times, then laughs. "Thanks for raising that point, Alex. When I say archaeology is garbage, I don't mean to be disrespectful. I'm a professional garbage collector, and I'm getting paid not very much money to entice you all to be garbage collectors too. If I didn't love what I do, I wouldn't be here.

"But I think it's very important to impress on you from the beginning that glamour is not what this is about. You need to be able to do painstakingly detailed work, keep scrupulous track of what you find, be conscious of your own biases—and always be ready to be surprised. I'll be preparing you for the 'surprise' part by giving some pop quizzes throughout the term."

Everyone groans. She smiles.

"I'm looking forward to teaching this class. I always do. And I also think it's important for you to know that I don't stop being available to you when the class ends. I've written lots of recommendations, and I'm delighted to give feedback about archaeology and anthropology programs at various colleges and universities. I know lots of people in this field. And I do answer my e-mail, although sometimes it may take a while."

Alex raises his hand again. Ms. Fraser nods. He asks, "Do you think the program at Harvard is worth anything these days?"

Good God, what a putz. He makes my stomach hurt. I always get embarrassed when I'm around people who have no idea how annoying they are. Ms. Fraser says, "You can come to me with questions about specific programs outside of class. We're too pressed for time as it is."

Nicely done! I smile at Ms. Fraser. Then I whisper to Anne, "Can you believe he even asked that?"

She whispers back, "Yes, unfortunately. He's from my school. We rode up together." She makes a face.

"Oh, I'm so sorry."

Anne adds, "His dad is just like him, only worse. I wanted to have my boyfriend drive me up, but John had to work. He's a lifeguard."

I immediately conjure up a mental picture of a beefy tanned guy with a whistle around his neck and a baseball cap on backwards, zinc oxide painted on his nose.

"Do you have a picture of him?" I ask, and Anne beams. I think I've just scored several points. She opens her neat gray leather purse, removes a matching wallet, and flips it open to reveal a picture of her in a severe black dress with her hair up, next to a guy in a white tux and black cummerbund. I would have thought he was her brother if I didn't know already that he was her boyfriend John the lifeguard.

"I miss him so much already," she whispers. "This was at Homecoming last fall."

I smile, deciding not to tell her that I think school dances are some of the most outrageous wastes of time and money that I can imagine.

Ms. Fraser clears her throat, from directly behind me. "Any other questions?" she asks. Anne and I blush and stop talking.

Ms. Fraser passes out the syllabus and tells us that she has a few extra copies of each book in case we didn't get a chance to order them before we got here, "or if you put them in that suitcase that got sent to Belize by mistake."

It's going to be more reading than anything else, and then discussion of what we've read. Good—I was nervous about the idea of actually digging up anything. I'm so clumsy that I'd probably end up falling into the trench onto some incredibly valuable artifact. I wonder if part of the training to be an archaeologist involves learning how not to do stuff like that.

"That's all I've got for you today. I'll see you tomorrow morning, and we'll talk about the first reading. Any general questions?"

I raise my hand.

"I don't know if you want to answer this, but what's the most interesting thing you've ever dug up?"

"You want me to give away my secret this early?" asks Ms. Fraser.

"Am I not supposed to ask until the fifth week?" I only talk like this to teachers when I'm very sure I'm going to get along with them. I'm kind of impressed that she caught us talking, actually. Teachers usually don't notice me doing anything besides raising my hand. Sometimes not even that.

"Well, maybe the fourth week. But I'll tell you part of the secret now: I haven't dug anything up, out of the ground—*but* I've discovered some fascinating artifacts. Bonus points to anyone who can figure out how I've done that. Tell me your guesses tomorrow."

Since Ms. Fraser let us out early, what I *should* do is start the reading for tomorrow. What I *want* to do is look for Battle and Katrina, but I think that would make me an eager little puppy dog tagging along after them. So I decide to practice viola instead.

I'm not that good of a viola player. I don't think there *are* many good viola players. Most of the ones I know are ex-violinists who weren't getting anywhere. I am the only person I know who wanted to start as a violist. That's probably why I'm first chair at school.

My viola feels warm when I take it out of its case, and I regret leaving it so close to the light from the window. I'll have to start keeping it under my bed. It takes forever to tune, and it will only get worse when it gets more humid. I jam the A-string peg as far in as possible, but I'm afraid that it's going to slip out of tune as soon as I let go.

As I'm struggling to tune the other strings, I look out of the window at the courtyard, which is full of trees, with a couple of benches at each end. There are some people I don't know playing Frisbee, and I think I see Kevin with some other guys playing Hacky Sack.

I turn away from the window, open my scale book, and start to play.

"Carl Sutter is a god in human form," announces Katrina at dinner, which is soggy but not entirely awful-tasting pizza. I wonder if I'll get so used to this swill that I won't be able to recognize good food when I get home.

"Who the hell's Carl Sutter?" asks Isaac.

"He's a genius, a snappy dresser, and, it just so happens, also the Computer Science teacher. You should really all drop what you're taking while there's still time to get in on the power and the glory that is Carl."

I say, "Hey Battle, my teacher said something in class today about discovering artifacts without digging them up out of the ground. Is she some kind of weird archaeological psychic?"

"Oh, she *is* the same one! She used that line last year, too." Battle looks pleased. She continues, "What she's talking about is a kind of archaeology—I don't remember the name—where you use metal detectors and other equipment to see what's in the ground at a site, but you don't disturb the artifacts."

"What's the point of that?" I ask, disappointed that the explanation isn't more exotic.

"Well, if you dig everything up and take it away, it's not a site any more. There's no context," Battle explains in her slow sweet voice.

"Oh, like a crime scene. If you disturb the body, you won't be able to solve the murder," says Isaac, taking his glasses off and rubbing his nose.

"Yeah, but that seems excessive. I mean, everything I know about archaeology is about people digging things up!" I say.

"This must be the politically correct kind of archaeology. You don't cut down the rain forest, so you don't dig stuff up, either," Katrina guesses.

"Speaking of politically correct, my teacher is Mikhail

Gorbachev," says Isaac. "Just kidding. Actually it's Ralph Nader. No, honestly this time—it's Richard Nixon, raised from the dead and ready for action!"

I laugh, but nobody else does. "Who is it really, Isaac?" I ask.

"Oh, some guy. I forget his name."

"So, not that good, huh?" I ask.

Katrina puts her hands over her mouth to make a megaphone. "Act now! Learn to make the computer obey your every command!"

"You're really into computers," says Isaac, with a note of wonder in his voice.

"You have a *problem* with girls being into computers?" Katrina demands.

"Uh oh, watch it, she's gonna take you out, man!" says Kevin in his deliberate way.

Kevin has spent the entire meal up to this point composing. At least, that's what I assume he's been doing, although it looks more like he's making a connect-the-dots version of a Jackson Pollock painting.

"No, I don't have a problem with it. I just think computers are boring. I don't know why anybody's into them." Isaac pulls all the cheese off his pizza and stuffs it into his mouth. Yuck.

"Well, you're an infidel," says Katrina, but she doesn't

sound angry any more. She starts explaining to him why he should care about computers, and I turn to Battle and ask, "So, what about your teacher?"

Battle says, "She's fine," as though I'd asked whether or not she was sick.

"Fine? Just fine? That doesn't sound very exciting. Are you going to get to study cool stuff, at least?"

"I like history," she says. It's not really an answer, but I don't seem to know how to ask her the right questions.

One of the Goth girls walks past our table. She's wearing an amazing black satin dress with a dark red velvet vest and incredibly high-heeled black leather boots. I smile at her to show my appreciation for the outfit.

"What the fuck's so fucking funny, bitch?" she says, and stalks off without waiting for me to reply.

Battle says, "Don't let her get to you. The Angst Crows are like that."

"Angst Crows?"

"That's what I called them last year. They were in Archaeology. All they ever wanted to talk about was burial practices."

"Oh, I think we have one of them this year, too. Do they like anybody?"

"Each other," says Battle.

"All I did was smile at her," I say.

Battle shrugs. "Some people think everyone wants to screw them over."

June 17, 8:30 a.m., Prucher Hall Lobby

They're taking us on a Hike today, I guess so that we don't shrivel up and die from studying too much. I love hiking, but I hate Hikes.

Katrina looks as though she's on her way to the electric chair. She is wearing a T-shirt with a smiley face on it, except that the face is frowning, and black leggings with a small white repeating pattern which, up close, is revealed as the word "Fuck" in tiny type.

"It's not as bad as it could be, y'all," says Battle. "They could be making us do one of those nasty trust things where we have to fall into each other's arms." She puts a hand to her forehead and pretends to swoon, catching herself right before she loses her balance.

"But I *do* trust you guys! I could do that all day! That wouldn't involve walking giant distances," says Katrina.

As soon as we get outside, we see Isaac and Kevin. Isaac has the exact same expression as Katrina. He's rubbing the lenses of his glasses maniacally with the tail of his shirt. It's as though he thinks that if he can just get them clean enough, when he puts them back on, he'll be transported to a place where Hikes are not required. Kevin looks like a page from some hip outdoor gear catalog. He says slowly, "I can't wait till we're out in the woods! All these buildings, they drag me down."

I look questioningly at the friendly brick facade of Prucher Hall, the only building in evidence. The courtyard that we're standing in is full of trees. Kevin and I are definitely not from the same planet. Meanwhile, Katrina is glaring and lighting a cigarette.

"Only you can prevent forest fires," says Isaac, waggling a finger at her.

"Or cause them. . . . Hey, now there's an idea! If the forest were on *fire*, we wouldn't have to walk in it, right?" asks Katrina, a demonic gleam coming into her eyes.

"That would be a Bad Idea," Battle says. She's holding her nose again. "You would damage the ecosystem. Plus they would figure out it was you, and then they'd expel you and you'd have to pay a truly enormous fine."

"Don't talk to me about ecosystems. Native Americans burned parts of forests all the time, and it was good for them," says Katrina.

"The Native Americans or the forests?" I ask.

"Both," Katrina says decisively.

It appears that Kevin has started to dance a peculiar

form of jig. Then I realize that he's only playing with his Hacky Sack.

Isaac looks at his watch. "Zero hour," he says.

The forest is actually quite small as forests go. It covers one large hill, which we will walk up and back down again for purposes of the Hike. The hill is so thickly covered with pine trees that from a distance it looks downy, like moss. It seems strange to think that there's enough space between the trees for us all to walk.

Ms. Fraser has asked us to bring back any signs of human habitation that we find—a sneaky way of getting us to pick up garbage.

"Carl says this is a waste of time and he doesn't know why they make us do it. He says it makes sense for *botanists* and people like that, but not for computer scientists." Katrina manages to make "botanist" sound like a swear word.

"Everybody should get outside more. John Cage said that the natural world was more inspiring than any other composer," says Kevin. Battle smiles at him.

All I know about John Cage is that he wrote some piece called *4'33"*, which is four minutes and thirty-three seconds' worth of silence. We're always trying to get our conductor to let us do it for one of our concerts.

We've joined up with the rest of the group now, at the foot of the hill. The RA in charge is saying something about being careful because the trail isn't always smooth, and how it should take a couple of hours each way.

I'm standing between Isaac and Battle. I edge a little closer to Battle and ask, "So what do you think of hiking?"

"I love it," she says, "but not in a crowd like this."

"I wish we could just do our own little hike," I say. I see the two of us walking quietly together in cool green shade, breathing in the scent of pine.

"Do you want to?"

"Now?"

"No, silly, we can't now. But some other time, do you want to?"

"Yes," I say. This is the first thing so far that Battle and I like and Katrina doesn't.

It's steep. I can feel my calf muscles working with every step. Eventually, our group splits up in a predictable way: Kevin far ahead, Katrina far behind, Isaac slightly ahead of her, and Battle and I almost in step in the middle.

I feel guilty about not being back with Katrina, but it's nice to walk with Battle. There are a lot of other people around, too, of course—the wood-chip-covered trail is wide enough across for six or seven people at a time—but no one else near us that I know. There are several RAs interspersed at various points, but they have stopped pointing out interesting ecological details as the difficulty of the climb has increased.

Battle doesn't get flushed, I notice enviously. I see just a few beads of sweat near her temples, near where her hair has started escaping from its ponytail. My own face is, I am sure, the exact color of a beet.

The trail dips down suddenly. I step too hard, my right foot slips, and the next thing I know, I am on the ground with pain shooting from my ankle.

Battle is kneeling next to me in an instant. "Are you okay?" she asks.

An RA appears, anxious and annoyed. "Don't try to walk!" he says angrily, as though I showed any signs of doing so. Meanwhile, Battle has started very carefully to unlace my shoe. My ankle is throbbing as though there's a second heart beating in it.

"Stop that," says Isaac, who has also showed up to peer at me. Suddenly I feel like everybody's science project. "If you take her shoe off, her foot will swell up too big to fit into it and she'll have a harder time getting back. I'm Red Cross certified in First Aid."

"You are?" the RA asks, as though Isaac has just said that he is God. "Can you get her back to the nurse's office? If I leave, we won't have enough adults . . . oh, shit, and I have to file an incident log. . . ." His voice trails off.

"Sure," says Isaac. "No problem. Where's your first aid kit?"

The RA blinks.

"Where there would be a *splint*—" Isaac is getting more insistent, "—to immobilize her *ankle,* so it won't get *worse?*"

As I look at the RA's face right now, I fully understand the expression "deer in the headlights." It would be hilarious if my ankle didn't hurt so much.

"You could use a couple of branches," Battle says quietly. "Here."

"And attach them with . . ."

". . . my jacket?"

Battle and Isaac start fussing with her jacket, the branches, and my ankle, trying to figure out the best place to secure the splint.

"You guys, I really don't think you need to do all this. I'm fine," I lie.

"Jesus Christ, what happened to you? I knew this whole hike idea was the spawn of Satan. Are you okay?" Katrina kneels next to me, getting her "Fuck" leggings dirty on the ground.

"She's not okay, she's sprained her ankle. I'm going to get her back to see the nurse," Isaac says.

Oh, is that what's happening?

"I'm really okay. Just let me stand up," I say. This is the kind of thing that happens to me all the time: some incredibly embarrassing, entirely stupid accident which reveals that the mere act of walking is apparently too difficult for me to grasp.

They don't let me stand up until they've finished the splint, and when I do, all the pain comes back, and I almost lose my balance. All three of them reach out for me at the same moment, but Isaac is the closest. He keeps me from falling by grabbing me around the waist and putting one of my arms over his shoulders. We are close enough to the same height that he only has to bend over a little to make a good crutch.

"Do you want help getting back?" asks Battle.

"Yeah, we could, like, take turns carrying you or something!" says Katrina.

"You couldn't lift me," I mumble. At the same time, Isaac says, "No, you go on, I think we'll be okay."

My ankle hurts. "Let's just *go*," I say.

"Make them give you some great painkillers! Then we'll have a party!" says Katrina.

Battle is already continuing up the hill, I notice. She turned away from us right after I said that I wanted to go. It's almost as though my saying that made her angry.

"Does it feel like you broke any bones?" Isaac asks, as we start awkwardly back down the trail with everyone staring at us.

I shake my head. "I don't think so," I say, "but I haven't broken any before, so I wouldn't know. Why are you Red Cross certified, Isaac?"

Isaac tries to shrug and then remembers that he's being a crutch. "It's dumb," he says. "My parents want me to be a doctor, right? *Blah blah blah my son the doctor.* And you can't send your kid to med school when he's fifteen, so what's the next best thing?"

"Oh, I get it. Did you hate it?"

"No. I really liked it, but I wasn't about to tell that to the parents. *Parents,*" he says, as though I should understand immediately what he means.

After a moment or two, I have an honesty attack. "Actually, I like mine."

"You're lucky," says Isaac. He sounds almost sad.

We walk—well, he walks, I limp—in silence for a while, and my mind drifts.

Why didn't Isaac want Battle and Katrina to help take me back? It's obviously Katrina that he has the crush on, so it's not like he wanted to, like, get me alone or something. Was it some macho boy kind of "I know First Aid and you guys don't" thing?

"Do you need to rest?" Isaac asks.

"No."

The nurse failed to give me any painkillers suitable for recreation, but I did get a large number of cold packs, of which Katrina highly approves. "Functional, yet stylish, in a very 'now' shade of electric blue!" she says, putting one on her head.

"Don't ruin that, she's going to need it," warns Battle.

Katrina brought me extra pillows and candy.

Battle gave me a flower that she picked at the top of the hill. "Since you didn't get to see the whole field of them, I thought you should at least have one."

"Thanks for coming to see me, you guys," I say. "I felt like such a moron for falling like that."

Katrina says sarcastically, "Yeah, well, we were meaning to speak to you about that, you know, we just don't want to be seen with someone who's always getting *injured,* it's just so uncool." She rolls her eyes.

"I fell off the stage once during a dress rehearsal," says Battle. "I had all these complicated things to do with my arms, and I completely lost track of where my feet were. Everyone laughed."

"Really?" I ask. I can't imagine Battle ever doing anything ungraceful.

"Of course, I was five at the time," she adds with a little smile.

Before I can start to feel embarrassed again, Katrina starts talking. "You know . . . I bet, Nic, because of what happened to you, they won't make next year's group *go* on a Hike. What a noble sacrifice you made! You should be very proud."

After they leave, I write in my notebook.

isaac = smart, sweet, funny, cute but not too cute, super nice to me. all logic demands that i should have a crush on him.???

. . . i wish i knew the name of that flower.

June 22, 8:27 p.m., My Room

It seems like the point of this article on typology is that when archaeologists find pottery shards or whatever, they organize them somehow into different categories.

What I don't get is how they know where each one belongs. I mean, say you find this shard that has a pattern of wavy red and white lines. Why would you necessarily say that it has anything to do with a shard that has wavy *green* and white lines? Maybe the green meant something totally different. Maybe the red ones were only used on special occasions. Or maybe women used the red ones and men used the green ones. I just don't understand how you decide where something fits.

I stare at the words on the page until they turn into gibberish.

Battle had Archaeology last year. She must have

learned about typology. Or should I ask Anne? No, she probably won't have understood it either. Besides, I don't know where her room is, and if I tried to walk there my ankle would start hurting before I found it. And I bet she's on the phone with her lifeguard boy anyway.

Battle's room is just down the hall. It has a sign on the door which says, "All hope abandon, ye who enter here," with a picture of a three-headed dog. Battle made the three-headed dog picture on her computer, which of course Katrina was delighted to hear. Two of the heads are the actual heads of her dogs. The third head is the two of them morphed together in some complex electronic way.

It's kind of odd that I haven't seen Battle's room yet. But she's only been to mine when she and Katrina came to see me after I hurt my ankle. Mostly the three of us gather in Katrina's because she always wants to smoke, and Battle and I refuse to have her do it in our rooms.

I knock on the door. After a moment, Battle opens it. She smiles, and her eyes look even greener than usual. She's twisted her hair into a bun, which is secured with two pencils.

"Hi, are you busy?" I ask.

She shakes her head. "Come on in," she says. "Look at my shrine to Dante and Beatrice!"

Almost the whole wall behind her desk is covered with pictures of her dogs. The dogs running around in a big manicured yard, the dogs asleep on what must be Battle's bed back home, the dogs just standing around randomly looking adorable. "I miss my doggies," she says.

"I would never have guessed," I say.

She smiles. "Do you have a dog?" she asks.

I shake my head. "I had a goldfish once, but it died. And I guess you could say I have partial custody of my friends' cat, Frank."

Battle's room is terrifyingly clean. There are no clothes on the floor, the bed is made, there are no empty pop cans or candy bar wrappers. Even her books are in a neat pile on her desk, not scattered throughout the room on every available surface in Katrina's and my preferred method of organization. Her parents must love her.

"Which is which?" I ask, looking at the dog pictures.

"Dante is the sweet one. Beatrice is more troubled, she's a little worrier." Apparently Dante is just slightly taller, and has darker markings around his face. I still can't tell them apart when she's done explaining.

"Sit down," she says, gesturing at the bed.

"I like the floor," I say, and then regret saying it, because in order to lower myself to the floor without hurting my ankle, I have to stick my bad leg out in front of me in what looks like a bizarre martial arts move. "Um, so the reason I came over is that I'm really confused about this article, and I thought maybe you remembered it from last year."

Battle sits down next to me and flips through the photocopied pages. "It doesn't look familiar," she says. "I don't think we read it. But what was confusing? Maybe we read something like it."

I explain my problem with the whole concept of typology.

"I remember now," Battle says. "It bugged me too. The way they divided things into categories was so arbitrary—like the book would say that such-and-such design was a fertility motif, and how do they know?"

"Exactly! That's my exact problem with it. It makes me think—this is going to sound stupid—but do you ever have the feeling that everybody's making everything up, all the time? Like when a teacher tells you something is the absolute truth, and then later you learn it was just completely his opinion?"

Battle nods vigorously. "It's not just school. People ask my dad for advice, because he's a minister. I know he just says whatever comes into his head. But they think he's this grand authority."

"It's like there are all these people who want to be told what to do, and then there are people who want to tell them what to do—" I say, and Battle continues, "—and then there are people like us. We want to know *why* they're telling us to do it!"

Her green eyes are shining. *People like us,* I think, and I feel myself heat up, not in an embarrassed way, but in the way you feel when you walk into a warm room when you've been out in the cold for hours.

Battle pulls the pencils out of her hair and it falls in waves. She looks like a painting in one of Dad's art books. I realize I haven't said anything for a minute, and my mouth feels suddenly dry, and I start coughing. Then I feel like I have to say something, so I blurt out the first thing that comes into my head: "Has your dad always been a minister?"

"Did I sound like I was preaching?"

"No! I was—I was just curious."

Battle sighs and twists a lock of hair around her finger. "He used to be an actor. But he was always telling us that a pulpit was the best stage."

"Us?" I ask.

Battle gets up and walks over to her desk. She opens the middle drawer, takes out a small wooden box, and removes something from it, which she conceals in her hand. Then she hands me the box.

"Should I open it?" I ask. She nods.

Inside is a picture of a boy. Oh no. This must be her boyfriend.

"Have you been together for a long time?" I ask.

"We grew up together," Battle says in a strange high squeaky voice, "but I haven't seen him in a *long* time."

I tear my eyes away from the picture to look at her. On her right hand is a grinning boy puppet, wearing a bright red robe and a small gold crown. "A long time," she repeats in her real voice.

"You see," she says, again in the puppet voice, "once upon a time there was a little girl," she makes the puppet point to her face, "a little boy," the puppet points at the box, "and their mother and father. They were very happy." The puppet claps its hands. "They sang songs! They read stories! And they put on plays, on their special little stage." The puppet bows.

"Things changed when the father found God. He liked it more if the stories and songs and plays were from the Bible. And then the little boy didn't want to play anymore. He would say," she lowers the puppet voice to a growl, "'Don't expect me to take your shit forever,' and, 'You know nothing about who I am,' and 'When I'm seventeen, I'm gone.'"

She takes the puppet off and hands it to me. "And he was. I mean, he left. When he turned seventeen."

I think about putting the puppet on my own hand, but I don't feel I have the right. It's beautifully made, with a lot of detail in the features, and the red robe is a heavy velvet. "And you were close," I say, touching one of the points of the puppet's crown.

"Obviously not that close, since he hasn't bothered to

write me, or call, or send up smoke signals," Battle says, looking at her dog pictures. I think she's wishing they were here.

"Do you know where he is?"

She shakes her head. "He would talk about big cities all the time. San Francisco, New York, Los Angeles—he hated where we live. But I don't know which of them he picked. Or if he stayed wherever he went first. Basically, I don't know a damn thing."

Her smile is tight with pain. I want to say something to make it go away, but my brain is trying to do too many things at once, and all I can think of is "I'm sorry."

She shrugs. "It's not your fault. I'm sorry I brought it up, it's too intense for people to deal with."

"I'm not people," I say, hearing *people like us* in my head again. "I'm me, and I'm glad you told me about— what's his name?"

She smiles, and it's not quite so sad this time. "That's the funny part. His name is Nick."

"So that's why you looked at me so funny that first day when I said my name!" I say.

Battle blushes. "Was it that obvious?"

I nod.

"I'm sorry. It was just—well, he drew, too. He used to do all the backdrops for our stage. So, there you were, and you drew like him, and you had his name. . . ."

Her face changes.

"Don't tell anyone about this. Any of it. The last thing I need is for people to think I'm some poor little . . . just don't."

"All right, I won't."

"I have a lot of reading to get done," says Battle, quickly picking up a book from her desk.

"I'll go," I say. My ankle twinges when I stand up, and I wince.

"Will you be okay? I mean with your ankle? I sprained mine last year before our dance recital, I remember how much it hurt. . . ." Battle looks worried, which makes me feel somehow better.

"Yeah, don't worry about it."

Will you be okay without your brother?

June 24, 1:24 p.m., Student Services Office

"Maybe Mom and Dad will have sent me another cool postcard," I say. The last one was from a town in Ohio where they have the world's largest picnic basket.

"Yeah, and maybe *my* mom and dad will have sent me money!" says Isaac, rubbing his hands together in anticipatory greed.

"Like you can really *buy* anything around here," says Kevin in his deliberate way, bouncing his Hacky Sack off the wall near Battle's head. She glares at him, and he giggles.

I remember that Mozart was supposed to have been really annoying. I wonder if this means that Kevin is truly a genius composer. I hope not.

Only Isaac and I turn out to have mail. My postcard reads:

"Dear Nic—

"I'm trying to sell out, but nobody's buying. I'm considering setting up as a mall caricaturist."

Then there's a hideously grinning sketch of Dad's idea of a typical mall crawler—a woman with big hair, big teeth, and dangly earrings.

"On the bright side, the bleak artistic outlook means I can spare some time to see my only daughter for that parent weekend. Love, Dad."

Then there's a P.S. in Mom's handwriting.

"He's lying—it's going very well. But we are still going to be able to visit you. Hope you're well and not working too hard. Love you, Mom."

"Wow, my parents are coming for Parents' Weekend after all," I say, trying to figure out what I think about this idea. Battle looks at me questioningly, and I shrug.

"So are mine," says Isaac. His voice is flat and strange.

I look over and see that his hands are clutching his letter so tightly that the paper looks like it's about to rip in half.

"What's up?" I ask. Isaac shakes his head.

"It's not even worth mentioning." He crumples the letter, aims it at the wastebasket next to the desk and misses. Then he turns away from us and starts walking outside.

Battle, Katrina, and I all look at each other, and then at Kevin, who as the only other guy should be able to interpret this behavior. Kevin says, "Better leave him alone. Hey, I need to work out some chord progressions. See you guys later." Without waiting for us to answer, Kevin starts walking away, too.

The three of us look at each other again.

"Wow," says Katrina. She lifts up her right arm and sniffs experimentally under it a couple of times. "Did I forget my deodorant?"

After a moment, she walks over next to the wastebasket and picks up the crumpled ball of Isaac's letter.

"You know you want to," she says by way of justification. She uncrumples it and smooths it out.

Battle and I read over her shoulder:

"Dear Son:

"While you've been away at camp, your mother and I have been doing a lot of thinking. We have something to tell you. It won't be easy on any of us, but in the long run, you'll see that it's the best thing for everybody.

"*Your mother and I are getting a divorce.*"

That part is all typed. Then there's a part that's handwritten.

"*Sweetie, we don't know any of the details yet. Of course, we'll see you at Parents' Weekend and we can talk about all this. You need to start thinking about where you and your sister want to live, with your father or with me. You should have that choice. Love, your mother.*"

We are quiet for several minutes.

"His dad didn't even bother to sign it," I say softly.

"We've got to go talk to him. He must be going completely bugfuck, don't you think? Where do you think he is?" Katrina looks around as though Isaac might be lurking in a corner somewhere.

I shake my head. "But he said it wasn't even worth mentioning. I don't think he's going to want to talk anytime soon."

Battle says, "If he doesn't talk about it, it will drive him nuts. I know what I'm talking about." Her voice is quiet but insistent.

"What we need," says Katrina, "is a way to somehow *allow* him to talk without feeling like he's a loser just because his parents are screwing him over."

"But isn't he going to be furious that we read the note in the first place?" I ask.

Katrina shakes her head. "Why do you think he missed the wastebasket?" she asks.

"Um, maybe because he was really upset?" I offer.

Katrina shakes her head again. "It was because he wanted us to read the note. He wouldn't tell us about it directly, but he made sure we could find it," she says with absolute assurance.

"What do you think we should do, Nic?" asks Battle, looking at me seriously. I'm blushing. Again. Damn it. *Whatever* you *think*.

"Well," I fumble, "I guess what I think is that we should give him *some* time just to be upset by himself. I think we should talk to him, you're totally right, but after he's had some time to, you know, cool off."

"Point one," says Katrina, holding up her index finger, "the problem with Isaac, just like I was saying, is not that he needs to cool off. The problem is that without some intervention, he will freeze over completely." She has already started walking toward the door. "Point two," she holds up another finger, "is that regardless, he'll have some time to do that, because we don't know where the hell he is."

Why does Katrina think she knows Isaac so well? "I know where he is," I say. "Or at least I think I do. He likes walking by the river."

Katrina spins around to look at me for a minute, as though I've said something far more surprising than I think I have. Then I kick myself. I probably sounded like I had some kind of inside track to Isaac, which, if she's interested in him, which I think she is, would make her think that maybe I had a prior claim, or something.

"He said that when we were in the nurse's office waiting for her to look at my ankle," I explain.

I don't tell them what the nurse said. I guess we must have looked like we were really enjoying our conversation, because when she was done with the person before us, the first thing she asked was, "Are you here for birth control?" We burst into embarrassed laughter, and Isaac said, "No, pain control," and pointed to my ankle.

"So how are we going to do this?" asks Katrina. "Just waltz on up to him and say 'Hey, big guy, share your pain'?"

I say, "Maybe if we had some other excuse to be at the river. A picnic? We could get a bunch of candy and stuff from the machines."

"You can't go to the river," says Battle, suddenly sounding almost angry. "What about your ankle?"

"The nurse said it was only a mild sprain," I say. "It's a lot better."

"Fine, just reinjure it, then." It unnerves me to see Battle toss her hair back in a manner I can only describe as Imperious Cheerleader.

"It's Nic's ankle. I think she's the one who knows whether or not it's okay," Katrina says. Battle glares, but says nothing.

We acquire a variety of items from the vending machines. The four basic food groups are represented: caffeine, sugar, salt, and fat. "It'd be better if we had alcohol," Katrina says as she stows cans of soda in her army knapsack. "In wine is truth!"

"Oh, that'd be just what he needs," Battle says, "to get wasted when he's already upset."

Katrina shakes her head. "Jeez, go all 'just say no' on me, why don't you, preacher's daughter?'"

"Shut up," says Battle, walking away. She stays ahead of us all the way to the river. *My ankle only hurts a little,* I want to tell her.

When we find Isaac, the first thing I see is that he's torn up all the grass around where he's sitting. Lumps of grass and dirt are everywhere.

"Hi! We're having a picnic!" Katrina says brightly.

"Have it somewhere else."

I'm ready to leave. Then Battle says, "We read the letter. Be mad if you want, but we thought you might want to talk." Meanwhile, Katrina hands him a Ding Dong and a can of Coke.

Isaac opens the Ding Dong package and peels the chocolate off the top. Then he rolls it up like a cigarette and puts the tip of it in his mouth.

"Hey, light this one up for me, Katrina," he says. He sucks it all the way into his mouth, loudly.

Battle sits down, carefully avoiding the area Isaac has devastated.

"Do you want us to leave?" asks Katrina.

Isaac suddenly looks different, in a way I can't quite define. It's as though he's actively shaken off one mood and is trying desperately to put another one on.

"No—I was just kidding before. You can have your picnic or whatever." He wipes off the chocolate crumbs from around his mouth and gulps down some Coke.

"So did you know this was coming?" Battle asks.

"You guys? No, otherwise I would have had, you know, a picnic blanket all laid out."

Battle glares. "Not us. The divorce."

Isaac takes a long sip of Coke. "Ah, the breakfast of champions," he says.

Katrina and I sit down. I pick up one of Isaac's dirt-grass lumps and start pulling on individual strands of grass, trying to see if I can pull one all the way out without it snapping.

"Were they fighting a lot?" Battle persists.

Isaac takes a huge bite of Ding Dong and says, muffled through it, "Oh no, they were in total and perfect harmony every moment, exhibiting great parenting skills to me and my baby sister. Jesus, what do you think?"

"Do you have any idea where you want to live yet?" I ask.

"Yeah. Not with either of them."

The dirt-grass lump crumbles in my hands. Now my hands are all covered with dirt, and I don't have anything to wipe them on but my shorts. I'd rather not. I don't want to look any sloppier than I do already. I rub my hands together and get most of the dirt off, but they still feel gritty.

"And I have to write this fucking position paper, and something's fucked up with my word processor," says Isaac, looking at Katrina.

"Not for long," she says. "Geek girl to the rescue!" Then her face turns an intense shade of pink, and she adds quickly, "You guys come too, you might learn something."

Judging from his expression, a crowd scene was not what Isaac had in mind. But he doesn't say anything as we all troop back to Prucher Hall to go up to his room. I wipe my hands off on my shorts when Battle's not looking.

We're not ever supposed to be on the guys' hall, officially, but Isaac and Kevin have both mentioned that their RA doesn't seem to be capable of noticing anything short of a nuclear attack. The gossip is that he is trying to use this summer to write his master's thesis, and so all he does is sit at his computer with his headphones at top volume.

But unfortunately, the RA seems to be taking a break. He's standing in the hallway outside his room as we approach, and he says, "Hey, where are you all going?"

"Study group," says Katrina promptly. "Isaac has the notes we need on his computer."

The RA wrinkles up his face in thought. "I guess that's all right. Just leave the door open, okay?"

We all nod seriously. But when we get to Isaac's room, we can't help cracking up.

"For God's sake, don't close the door, because if you did, we would just all be compelled to have sex with you immediately," says Katrina. "He must think you are a *major* studboy!"

"And you don't?" Isaac challenges.

She says very quickly, in a higher voice than usual, "Yeah, he must have been having visions of all *kinds* of goings-on—ooh, step back now, I'm going to boot up your *hard* drive. . . ."

I suppose I shouldn't be surprised that Isaac hasn't decorated his room at all. The only things identifying the room as his are the clothes and books on the floor. Suddenly he blushes and kicks a pair of underwear underneath the bed.

Battle and I sit on clear parts of the floor. Katrina sits cross-legged in Isaac's chair and peers at his computer screen. Isaac hovers close by her.

"I've got it," she says after a few minutes, "you moved your Office Folder into Queries, so nothing will—"

She's interrupted by the sound of Isaac's phone ringing.

We stare at it as it rings, all obviously thinking the same thing: that it's one of his parents. It keeps ringing, and it doesn't seem like the person on the other end is going to hang up any time soon, so Isaac sighs and grabs the receiver.

"Hello? Oh hi."

Pause.

"I've been busy. This is an intensive program, you know."

Pause.

"What do you mean, have I met anybody? Of course, I've met tons of people—my class alone has twenty-five people in it."

Katrina raises one eyebrow. "Girlfriend," she mouths, and Battle nods. We get up.

Isaac says, "Don't go." Then he says into the phone, "No, not you. I've got some people in my room." We sit back down.

Pause. Isaac starts to hold the phone some distance away from his ear, although the voice on the other end is not getting any louder. Then he puts his mouth close to the receiver again and says, "Yeah, I know. Yeah. Listen, I can't talk much longer. I don't want to run your phone bill up."

Pause.

"Yeah, I know your dad pays it. I've gotta go."

He hangs up.

"Harsh," says Katrina.

"It was nobody important," says Isaac.

"Dang, I guess not," says Battle.

The phone starts ringing again.

"Let it ring," says Isaac.

"It must be hard to concentrate on anything right now," I say, speaking more loudly than usual to be heard over the phone.

"I don't even know what they're doing with me and Rebecca," Isaac says with a kind of outrage in his voice. Then he unplugs the phone.

"Rebecca's your sister?" I ask.

"Yup. She's ten. You'd like her," he says to Katrina. "She's a lot like you."

Katrina blushes for no apparent reason. Then she asks, "Are they going to do one of those 'Dad gets the boy, Mom gets the girl' things?"

Isaac opens a desk drawer and slams it shut. "They'd better not."

"One of them might want to move away," Battle suggests quietly.

Before Isaac can respond, Katrina jumps in. "That's exactly what happened with my ma, she couldn't get far enough away from my dad. It sucked having to leave New York, but I was already kind of in the middle of an identity shift, and then when we got to Santa Fe, nobody knew anything about who I was before, so I got to be whoever I felt like being."

I wonder what Katrina was like before her parents got divorced. I wonder how she dressed. Right now, she's wearing a white Oxford cloth shirt over a blue glitter tube top, a Catholic-school-uniform-looking green and red plaid skirt, and purple motorcycle boots. And she has glow-in-the-dark plastic skeleton earrings.

Meanwhile, Isaac is pondering the new identity idea.

"I'll be a jock—drink lots of beer and treat women like shit! Oh, wait—to be a jock you have to have athletic ability. Damn."

We're laughing. Isaac continues: "I'll grow my hair out and get a guitar and write sensitive songs about love and death and the fate of the planet. Being completely tone-deaf wouldn't get in the way, would it?" He pauses to gulp down more Coke, and then goes on: "Now I've got it! I'll wear badly fitting clothes, overeat, carry a really thick book, and hold forth about the continuity problems on last week's *Star Trek*! That always gets the chicks."

"Ooh, baby—the thicker the better!" says Katrina.

Battle and I shriek, and Isaac says, "What'd I tell you?"

"The *book*! I meant the *book*! Jeez, you guys!" Katrina grabs a pillow from Isaac's bed, throws it at him, and misses. He hurls it back, and it hits her right in the head.

"I dunno, Battle—I think we ought to leave," I say, grinning.

Battle says, "You got that right." We get up and start for the door.

"Bye, guys!" calls Isaac, scooping up the pillow in preparation for another strike. "Come back any time!" He starts to close the door. Then Katrina pushes past him and says, "Let's talk more later—right now I need to have a serious discussion with my girls here."

Isaac's face falls. I'm the only one who sees it, though. He closes the door.

Katrina starts in on us immediately, although she can't keep from laughing.

"Very funny, you two. I say *one* thing—just *one thing*—"

I say, "Katrina, just face it. He's hot for you." Battle nods.

Katrina rolls her eyes. "That is *so* unlikely. You heard him—I remind him of his friggin' baby *sister!* It'd be about as likely as the three of *us* getting the hots for each other."

"Bye, you guys—see you soon," I say, and put the receiver down. My ear is warm. I must have been on the phone with Mom and Dad for over an hour.

I don't remember anything they said.

Or anything I said.

Earlier tonight, I tried to write my objective description for class tomorrow. Ms. Fraser said that we could describe anything: an object, a place, a person—the only requirement was that whatever we chose had to exist in the world somewhere, it couldn't be made up. It's supposed to teach us how important it is to be unbiased when you're describing an artifact.

I always write things out in longhand before I put them on the computer, so the ripped-out page from my notebook is still crumpled into a ball on the bed.

I was just about to tear it up when the phone rang. I pick it up, uncrumple it, and look again at what I wrote.

Battle Hall Davies is sixteen. She lives in North Carolina. She has long blonde hair and eyes the color of leaves in spring. She is 5'7" or 5'8". She wears jodhpurs and riding boots, not because she has a horse, but because she likes the style. ~~She has a brother.~~ She has two dogs named Dante and Beatrice.

Most of the time, she speaks slowly, as though each word is important and deserves its own moment. When she speaks fast, it means she's especially excited, or angry.

She rarely blushes. When she does, it makes me think of early morning, when the light is pale and the sky ever so faintly pink. ~~(It's nothing like the overripe tomato of some people's faces when they blush.)~~

When she laughs at something I say, I feel more funny and more smart than I ever have in my life. ~~When she smiles~~

She bites the skin around her cuticles, like I do. When I see blood on one of her fingers, I have the crazy urge to press one of my wounded ones up against it, so our blood will mix.

Stop.

This is not objective. This is not good scientific practice.

Infatuation is not good scientific practice.

My hands shake as I read those words again. Stupid, stupid, stupid.

I crumple the paper, uncrumple it again, then rip it into tiny pieces.

Realize that now I have to describe something else for tomorrow.

Open viola case. Write lame description of viola. Close viola case.

Realize that I will spend the rest of the night staring at the ceiling.

Last year, during *Guys and Dolls,* I was stage manager. I had to help Rachel, who was playing Sarah, with her costume change before the Havana scene. It was a quick change, so I held her fancy dress while she wiggled out of the skirt and unbuttoned the jacket of her Salvation Army uniform. Standing there in her lacy underwear and bra, she looked like a pinup girl from the forties—the kind of girl who'd be painted on the side of an airplane that shot down Nazis.

She stepped into the fancy dress and pulled it up, and I went behind her to zip it. "Oh my god this is tight," she said. "Does it make me look fat?"

"No," I said. "You look beautiful."

She kissed me on the cheek and said, "You're such a sweetheart, Nic!" before sailing out onto the stage.

Margaret, who'd been putting the props in order, came

up behind me and mimicked, "Ooh, you're thuch a thweet-heart!" Then in her real voice: "I saw you staring. You're just a little thespian lesbian, aren't you?"

I think I said, "Fuck off," or something equally brilliant, but the words kept echoing in my head, and I almost missed calling three light cues in a row.

But that's not the whole story.

I see beautiful Rachel in my head, but then I see shy, smart André—the boy I spent all last year in Geometry try-ing desperately to attract.

It doesn't make sense. *Thespian lesbian, thespian les-bian.* How can I be a thespian lesbian when I filled up a whole notebook with ways to impress André?

Then André's face turns into Battle's, and I wish I could stop seeing her, wish I could stop thinking about what it would feel like just to touch her hair or hold her hand.

But I can't.

field notes:
    i tried to press that flower battle brought me from the hike, but it didn't dry, it just squished like a dead bug. i hope this is not an ominous sign from above.

66

July 3, 11:30 a.m.,
Parents' Weekend Brunch

Sometimes I think the reason I like archaeology so much is that it's all *over*. I can analyze artifacts for the rest of my life, and in the grand scheme of things, if I put a clay pot together the wrong way, or decide that something was a weapon when it was actually a hairpiece, it won't matter. Not to anyone alive.

Dealing with people is messier.

The seating chart, clockwise: me, Battle, her mom, her dad, Katrina's mom, Katrina, Isaac, Isaac's mom, Isaac's dad, my dad, my mom.

(Kevin's parents couldn't come, so he's probably off composing twelve-tone chants. Or playing Hacky Sack. Or both.)

It makes my stomach hurt to see Isaac's parents. They look alike, two short, dark, lumpy people, more like brother and sister than husband and wife. And they both look exhausted, as though they haven't slept well for months or even years. They don't look at each other. They don't speak to each other, either, unless it's absolutely necessary.

I look at Battle's parents, instead. Her dad's hair is a deeper gold than hers, his eyes are hazel, and his skin is weathered—he could be the illustration for "distinguished" in the dictionary. Actually, he looks exactly like an actor playing a minister in a movie, which I guess isn't far from the truth, except that presumably, he really *does* have some kind of calling.

Battle's mother is perfectly put together. Her makeup is so artful you can hardly tell it's there, but there's a kind of sheen and polish to her features. Both of them are dressed as though they're in church, which of course is not surprising.

What *is* surprising is Battle.

Her hair is pulled back into the tightest French braid I've ever seen, and she's wearing a staid long pink dress that I've never seen before. She keeps peeling the skin from around her fingernails, and she's paying more attention to her napkin than to anyone at the table.

My parents look like they've been on the road for a month, which they have. Dad is wearing jeans and one of his trademark black T-shirts (they don't show the ink-stains), and Mom is wearing what I have christened the Sack Lunch Dress: it's shapeless and the exact brown of a brown paper bag.

Katrina and her mom look alike, except that Katrina's mom has a lot of gray in her hair and dresses slightly less flamboyantly.

Before anyone starts talking, Battle's father bows his head, laces his fingers together, and speaks very quietly for a while. It takes me a minute to realize that he must be saying grace, and then I feel sort of sheepish for being such a heathen. But no one except Battle's mother seems to be paying any attention to him, so I don't either.

Our first topic of conversation, courtesy of Isaac's father, is the ham croquettes.

"This is a slap in the face!" he says.

"Dad, we've never kept kosher in our lives," says Isaac.

"Hey, that means more for the rest of us! They look great!" says Katrina's mom amiably.

"Probably even better with ranch dressing, Ma." Katrina takes a croquette.

After a moment, so does Isaac. He eats his croquette with exaggerated relish, and I find myself thinking about the cigarette he tried to smoke for her. At least there's not a wrong way to *eat* something.

"Hey, do you think they have *cheese* sauce for these?" Isaac asks of no one in particular.

"I find fruit salad so refreshing on hot days like this, don't you?" asks Battle's mother, passing the chilled bowl to Isaac's dad, who scowls at it.

"Oh, yes, I do," says Isaac's mom, taking the bowl away from her soon-to-be-ex-husband. "Isaac, take some fruit, you never eat enough fruit." She heaps some onto his plate and adds in an undertone, "He'd have scurvy if it wasn't for Tang."

"Didn't you say you've got a younger sister?" Katrina demands. Isaac's mother says, too cheerfully, "How sweet of you to ask! She's staying with their aunt—she's having a hard time just now, you know how it is—do you have brothers and sisters?"

Katrina shakes her head. "They broke the mold."

My mom says, "Nic's also an only child."

"Wow! Well, aren't we just the poster table for zero population growth! You, too?" Katrina's mom looks at Battle. Battle opens her mouth, and her mother says, "That's right."

Battle shuts her mouth, so abruptly that I can almost hear her teeth click together. Then she pulls the pink elastic band out of her hair and spends the next several minutes carefully obliterating all traces of the French braid.

"Goodness, I wish you wouldn't do that while people are eating," says Battle's mother softly.

Even more softly, Battle says, "There are things I wish you wouldn't do, too."

I'm the only one who hears.

"What's that, dear?"

"I said I'm sorry, it was giving me a headache."

For a while, everyone eats quickly and silently, as though it's our last meal.

Then my dad starts telling lame stories about things that have happened while he and Mom have been traveling, and at the same time that I'm wincing and saying, "Oh, Dad," I'm realizing that his stupid jokes are putting the focus of the table's attention on him, and *because* everyone's focusing on him, it's diffusing all kinds of tension, and thinking about Dad doing that, on purpose, actually almost makes me want to cry.

After the brunch finally ends, Mom and Dad insist on driving me out to some big used bookstore they found on the way here, so I can pick out a present.

I can't think of anything I want.

Anything they can buy for me, anyway.

I scan titles, trying desperately to find one that I can pretend to be excited about. The science fiction section is lame. The only mystery that looks good is *Death Comes As the End*, but I've already read it.

The next section after Mystery is Pets. Why? Do all the little old ladies who pick up mysteries then feel compelled to get cat books?

Suddenly I see it—face-out on the shelf, with a photograph on the cover that could have come straight from Battle's wall. *All About Corgis*, it says in big friendly type.

"This one," I say, holding up the book for Mom to see.

"Really? Are you sure? I thought you hated dogs," Mom says.

"Positive," I say.

July 3, 8:47 p.m., My Room

<u>field notes:</u>

mom and dad left about an hour ago, and since they've been gone, i've been sitting on the bed, feeling homesick.

i think it's because i saw them that i'm homesick now. the siegel institute is its own, more intense world, and the intensity hasn't left me any time to think about home.

the most intense thing in my life has always (all right, for the last two years, anyway) been theater. i feel so much responsibility for every show. even back when i was just on props crew and the only thing i needed to do was make sure the typewriter case was prepped for act two in <u>glass menagerie</u>, i still felt like if i messed up, the entire show would be a disaster.

the times when i don't make any mistakes, when the actors are all on, and all the light cues and scene changes are going smoothly, there's a special quality to the air, like everyone on the show is getting twice as much oxygen with every breath.

but that feeling is nothing next to what i feel now about battle.

and it's stupid. i can't believe how mind-bogglingly, earth-shatteringly dumb it is. dumber than my crush on andré, even. at least with andré, i had every reason to suspect that i was of an appropriate gender to be involved with him. it's so dumb i can't even cry. all i can do is sit here on the bed with my knees drawn up to my chin, wondering what on earth i'm going to do with a giant stupid book about the kind of dogs she has.

There's a knock on my door. It's Katrina. "You're not doing anything, are you? I didn't think so. Listen, Mom brought me a *ton* of new and exciting chemically processed snack products, and I feel the need to share them with my loved ones, so come with me, we'll get Battle, go back to my room, and have a women-only riot!"

"Okay," I say, contemplating whether I should bring the dog book with me to give to Battle. It *will* reveal that I was thinking about her, which could be bad, but on the other hand, she seemed upset before and maybe the book will cheer her up. And it's a *book*, not a dozen roses, so it's not like I would be making some big declaration of love. I put it under my arm and we head to Battle's room.

"Who is it?" Battle calls through the door. Her voice sounds a little shaky.

"It's the Procrastination Police! Officer Lancaster and I

are here to make sure you don't get anything done tonight!" Katrina calls back.

"I'm so glad it's you!" Battle opens the door and crushes Katrina and me into a hug. I can barely breathe, mostly from nervousness, but I can tell that Battle smells like lavender. My favorite scent.

"Who were you expecting?" Katrina asks, plopping down on Battle's bed without a second thought.

My ankle only twinges a little when I sit down in the same spot on the floor as last time. "They said they were leaving, but I wasn't sure I believed them," Battle says.

"Your parents?" I ask. She nods.

"What was up with you this morning?" Katrina demands.

Battle shakes her head, and gives me a "don't say anything" glare.

I wasn't going to.

"They broke another promise," she says. "I don't know why I was even surprised. And then when Mom put my hair up—well, that's the way she wants me to be, all the time. Perfectly in order, and completely confined."

"What promise?" Katrina asks.

Battle shakes her head again. "They said it *cost* too much. I told them weeks ago that I'd pay. I told them how important it was to me. Money was just their excuse. It was really that it was *inconvenient* for them."

"What was? Oh, by the way, Mom and Dad took me to this bookstore and, uh, I thought you might like this." I hand the book to Battle.

"Thank—oh my god. How did you know?"

I gesture toward the dog-picture-covered wall.

"I mean about today—you didn't know about today?" She flips through the pages, then closes the book.

"Spit it out, Battle. We need some nouns here," says Katrina.

"The noun is dog. Plural, dogs. My parents promised they would bring Dante and Beatrice, and they didn't. Instead, they brought that *dress.*"

The dress, I notice, is on the floor in a heap. It's the only piece of clothing I have ever seen on her floor.

"And not only that." Battle gets up and walks over to her dresser. "Mom happened to let it slip that since I've been gone, they've been *boarding* them. Dante and Beatrice aren't even *home.*"

She puts the book down on the dresser, opens the top drawer and digs around in it. "I'm glad y'all are here, because I might need help with this."

Something metal flashes in her hand. "Battle?"

A wisp of her hair floats to the floor. Scissors, she's holding scissors—

"I'm shaving my head." Another wisp.

"Stop it!" I hear myself say.

"I want to do this, Nic, I've thought about it a lot," says Battle, cutting off a third wisp.

I go over to her, grab her wrist with my left hand, and take away the scissors with my right. "It can't be all random like that," I say, realizing that I'm using my stage manager voice. "You need to braid your hair first. Then you cut off the braid."

Battle rubs her wrist. "That hurt," she says.

Katrina jumps up from the bed and says, "Rock on, Nic! I wish we had a camcorder so we could capture it all on the magic of videotape! She's right, Battle—don't you think she's right?"

Battle nods, slowly. "Yes—but there's a problem." She seems embarrassed. "I can't braid my hair myself. You'd have to do it, Nic."

Katrina starts to say, "I can—" and I interrupt, "Fine. Get me a brush and a rubber band."

Battle hurries over to her dresser again, grabs the brush from on top of it, snaps open a small square tin and extracts a rubber band. She hands them to me like she's the nurse and I'm the surgeon.

"Sit at your desk chair," Stage Manager Nic commands. Battle does.

I move to stand behind her. There's her lavender scent again. Keep it together, Nic.

Her hair is silk. Heavy silk. Silk you could weave into a rope to cling to while you climbed a mountain.

The lavender makes me dizzy. No more stage manager. No more surgeon.

I am a lady-in waiting, and she is the princess. No, the empress. The empress of the world.

"Your Imperial Highness," Lady-in-Waiting Nic says, "do you truly think that shearing your golden tresses will foil the evil schemes of your deceitful parents, may they reign for a thousand years?"

"Nay, I fear not," the Empress Battle responds, picking it up immediately. "I wish only for them to see that I am not a doll to be dressed and played with."

"Indeed, you are no child's plaything, lady."

Divide it into three. Over, under, over. Gather more hair. Over, under, over. Finally, the rubber band. "Do you wish to inspect my handiwork before we proceed, Your Imperial Highness?"

Battle raises one hand regally to her head and carefully feels the braid. "It is well done. Now cut it off."

"My lady, wish you not to wield the blades yourself?" I pick up the scissors from the desk.

Battle shakes her head, just barely. "Nay, I do not wish it. Do me the honor of performing this service, and you shall be well rewarded."

"My lady, I wish no reward but to continue in your service."

I open the scissors, holding Battle's braid with my left hand. It takes me several cuts to get through the thick mass of hair. When I finish, I hold the braid in both hands for a minute. Then I go back around, still being Lady-in-Waiting, and kneel in front of Battle's chair, holding the braid out to her. "What is your will for this, lady?"

"You may keep it, if you desire. I have no further use for it," she says.

"Thank you, my lady!" We smile at each other.

"God!" Katrina says. "Would you guys get over yourselves? Isn't it time for the clippers yet? I can do that part, unless you would prefer that I just leave."

"No, no, that's fine—I mean, of course, you should do the clippers—um, they're in my dresser, I'll get them," says Battle all in a rush.

I have no idea what to do with Battle's braid. I don't want to throw it away, but I don't have any place to put it.

"I'll be right back," I say. "I'm going to get some soda. Want anything?"

"Coke, of course!"

"Sweet tea, or whatever they have that's closest."

"Okay. Don't cut off too much while I'm gone."

I go to my room and shove the braid into the bottom

drawer of my dresser, underneath a sweater Mom made me bring in case it got cold. Then I get the drinks and come back.

Katrina is doing stripes on Battle's head with the clippers, making race-car noises as she does it.

"Do you want this now, or do you want to wait till you're done?" I'm in the background again. Holding the props.

"Now!" Katrina takes the Coke, and Battle takes the bottle of frighteningly colored strawberry tea. I didn't get anything for myself, but they don't notice.

Battle runs her hands over her head and giggles. "I almost want to leave it like this," she says.

"That could work," says Katrina consideringly. "You could dye some of the stripes black, and it'd be this cool bumblebee effect."

Battle shakes her head. "No." She sounds serious again. "I can't do this halfway."

"Hon, excuse me for asking, but you don't actually think you're going to *accomplish* anything with this, do you? I mean, I totally am with you all the way, bald is beautiful and power to the people, but you don't, do you?"

Before Battle can answer, I say, "It seems like it's not about accomplishing something so much as it's about sending a message, is that right?"

"Exactly," she says.

"I just gotta get a message to yoo-oo-oo-oo," Katrina sings. "Let's finish it, then!"

Finishing it proves to be easier said than done. The clippers get clogged with tiny hairs, and we can't figure out how to take them apart.

"Maybe the last stage is Nair," suggests Katrina.

Eventually we decide that the last stage is a razor and shaving cream. We relocate to the bathroom down the hall and occupy one of the sinks. Fortunately, no one else seems to want to take a shower at eleven P.M.

This is the hardest part, and the least fun. It seems like every time Katrina thinks she's done, she discovers some new patch of stubble. Finally she steps away from Battle and says, "Nic, I think I'm starting to hallucinate hair that isn't there. Feel her head."

I wipe my hands on my jeans and tentatively put them on Battle's head.

"Your hands are like ice!" she says. Her voice sounds very loud.

"Sorry," I say, and immediately remove them.

"You don't have to take them away—it was just kind of a shock," she says quickly.

I put my hands back. Her head is warm, and her scalp is pink and looks a little raw. It feels smooth and strange. I move my hands over her head, feeling the skull underneath her skin, and I find myself wondering if my fingers will leave some kind of slimy track behind them, like ten snails.

I can hear her breathing—is it louder than usual? Faster? Or is that mine I hear?

I swallow a couple of times. I really should have gotten myself something to drink, too.

"I can't feel any hair," I announce, and step away.

I remember when I first saw Battle and thought of her as Beautiful Hair Girl. It seems so long ago. She's still beautiful, of course. But now she looks much more vulnerable. Smaller. It makes me want to protect her. I don't know from what.

"Ooh yuck, I have little tiny hairs all down my shirt," Battle says rapidly, in a higher voice than usual. She uses both hands to pinch her shirt at the shoulders, then shakes it in an attempt to dislodge the hairs.

"That's not gonna work, you'll have to take a shower," I say automatically. Then an incredibly vivid picture of Battle in the shower forms itself in my brain. Special effects, cue the Lancaster Special Neon Blush. Again? Yep, again.

"You're probably right. I guess I will," says Battle, after a moment. Did she look at me strangely before she said that? Oh, god. Please, let her not be able to read my mind.

"Get in the shower," says Katrina. "Nic, let's go to my room. I need another cigarette. That was hard work."

Katrina seems to have forgotten my part in the enterprise. I don't think I mind.

"Will y'all still be up when I'm done with my shower?" Battle asks.

"Are you kidding? The night is young! The riot has barely begun!"

"All right then."

Almost immediately after we leave the bathroom, Katrina says, "Nic, I'm going to ask you a question, and I want an honest answer. Would you have been happier if I left?"

"I—when?" I look intently at the carpet as we walk.

"You know when. When you were having your little balcony scene without the balcony. Should I have taken off?" Katrina sounds brusque, more New Yorkish than usual.

She unlocks the door to her room aggressively, and yanks it open, gesturing at me to go in before she does.

"I don't know," I say.

"Well, you better figure it out. I do *not* enjoy feeling like a third wheel."

"Katrina, I'm sorry—but I don't even know if there are two wheels for you to be the third of. I mean, I don't know if it's . . ." I don't want to finish this sentence, but now that I've started I can't stop: ". . . if it's just me."

"You mean you haven't done anything?" Katrina sounds shocked.

I shake my head. Katrina collapses onto her beanbag chair.

"God, Nic—I thought you two were having this secret dyke thing behind my back, and you didn't want me to know. I thought you thought I was this fucking homophobe or something."

I have the tightness at the back of my throat and the sting behind my eyes that means I'm going to cry. "I *wish*," I say. "I mean, not that it was happening behind your back—" I put my head in my hands. No tears come, yet.

"Oh, you poor thing!" Katrina launches herself out of the beanbag chair and hugs me. "Don't take that as a come-on," she says, giggling a little nervously.

"I won't," I say. "But listen, Katrina, I don't know—"

There's a knock on the door. Katrina and I step away from each other as though we've actually been doing something we didn't want to be caught at. "C'mon in!" says Katrina, and Battle walks in.

She's flushed from the shower, and her head is shiny.

I think about the braid in my drawer, underneath the sweater. The braid of Her Imperial Highness.

"How many cigarettes do you smoke in here?" Battle asks, coughing a little. "Isn't that against all the rules? Doesn't anyone ever—check on you?"

Katrina shakes her head. "My RA smokes, too," she says smugly. "I don't tell on her, she doesn't tell on me."

Battle sighs, and sits down next to me. She reaches over and takes one of my hands in both of hers. "Don't *you* start," she says, gripping my hand urgently.

"Um, I, I wouldn't dream of it," I manage to say, hoping that she can't feel the speed of my pulse.

"Good," she says, and drops my hand. Then she looks over at Katrina's Erté calendar. "I just remembered something. Isn't tomorrow the evil Fourth of July volleyball game?"

"Oh no," says Katrina, sounding genuinely stricken. "Oh god, I'd forgotten about that. What is it about this place that they think it's a good idea to force perfectly innocent youth to perform brutal and fascistic acts like hiking and playing volleyball?"

"Should we go to sleep, then? So we won't be totally wiped out when we have to get up to play?" I ask.

"Are you saying you would give up the joyous companionship of your loved ones for the sake of a game?" Katrina has her hands on her hips and is glaring at me.

I laugh, trying to catch her mood. "Okay, okay, forget I said anything. Bring on the chemically processed snacks!"

Katrina distributes various oddly shaped and colored sweets, including chocolate computer disks and chili-mango lollipops. I don't expect to like the lollipops, but I do. They come in two parts: the actual lollipop, which is purely mango-flavored, and a small, thimble-shaped container full of salt and chili powder, into which you dip the lollipop. There are also M&Ms. Katrina is about to dump them onto the floor when Battle the neat freak shrieks, "Put something down so they don't get ground into the carpet!"

Katrina obligingly produces an Indian cotton blanket, which she puts down without moving the books and clothes that are already on the floor. Then she pours out the M&Ms. I immediately begin to sort them by color. Katrina says, "No green ones for you!" She winks at me.

I could kill her, but two can play at that game. "Why not, are you going to save them for somebody? Like . . . Isaac maybe?" I ask, scooping up a handful of brown M&Ms and popping them into my mouth.

"Would you drop the Isaac thing? Even if I *was* interested, *which I am not,* he's totally freaked out about his parents, *and* he has a girlfriend back home!"

"I doubt that he does any more, after that phone call we heard, remember? Besides, he's probably going to end up moving, so that means he won't stay with her, right?" Battle asks.

"Oh, I see. He won't want a long-distance thing with her, but he will want one with me. Have I mentioned that you are totally delusional?" Katrina raps gently on Battle's shiny head.

"Maybe he'll end up moving to where you live!" I suggest, pleased that the focus of the conversation is now squarely on Katrina.

"Oh god. He'd fit right in. He could sell the traditional handicrafts of his people in the Plaza. Or perhaps he could attend services at one of our many fine Catholic churches—or, better yet, at a Mormon tabernacle!"

"My dad has a thing about Mormons," says Battle. "He says they should just become professional genealogists, since that's obviously where their talents lie, and leave the religion out of it."

"So do you have to go to church, like, every week?" asks Katrina.

Battle sighs. "Will you promise not to laugh?" she asks.

"No," Katrina and I say at the same time. Battle smiles wryly.

"Ha ha. Well, here's the deal. I have to go, but I don't attend the service. I take care of the babies that are too little to go to Sunday school. I read to them. Or sing."

Katrina says, "That is so adorable! I can just see you with a roomful of them. Especially now! 'Okay, kids, today we're going to make *hair* shirts!'"

Battle scoops up a big handful of M&Ms and puts them all in her mouth at once. Then she makes a horrible face that involves sticking her tongue out while it has a bunch of chewed-up M&Ms on it.

"Do you ever dance?" I ask. I picture Battle twirling gracefully through a room full of cribs and playpens, while all the babies watch with wide-open happy eyes, cooing and gurgling.

Battle shakes her head. "It's mostly about changing diapers."

Katrina says, "Hmmm . . . diapers. I don't know about that. But it's basically a nice dodge—it makes you look all virtuous, but you don't have to listen to the nonsense."

"Do you think it's all nonsense?" I ask. "My parents don't go, but sometimes I've gone with friends, and I don't know . . . so many people seem to get so much out of it."

Katrina says, "My dad's family are all real serious about it. My grandparents came and prayed over us once when Mom and Dad weren't divorced yet. They said something about holding onto the strength of the family. It just made me feel creepy. My mom stopped all that once she and Dad split up. I just live in fear that she'll hook up with some guy who'll be just as nuts for it as my grandparents are, and he and Mom will decide I need to be saved or something."

Battle sits up and takes a large gulp of Coke. "We're not going to sleep for days," she says, sounding rather pleased about the prospect.

"Does your dad talk about God at home?" I ask.

Battle shakes her head. "He writes his sermons in the study and we're not supposed to disturb him. And he goes and visits people sometimes in the evenings, like if some-body's dying, but he doesn't talk much about it to me and Mom. He doesn't really talk much about anything, when you get right down to it. But Mom makes up for that." She sighs.

"You know what I think about religion?" I ask. Not waiting for an answer, I say, "I think it would be great if it was all clear-cut the way it is in Madeline L'Engle books. Where you know who the bad guys are and it's all impor-tant and beautiful and it means that you can communicate telepathically with dolphins."

Katrina and Battle both burst out laughing. Katrina says, "Hey, sign me up! Bring on the dolphins!"

We sit for a while, munching candy and gulping soda. I can feel my heart rate speed up. I think the Coke is traveling directly through my veins. Then again, maybe I'm just ner-vous.

"I need a cigarette," says Katrina.

"Then you had best blow the smoke out the window, because I am *not* going to have my lungs blackened by your secondhand fumes," Battle announces.

Katrina says, "I told you I'm going to quit soon! It's just that things are kind of stressful right now. I want to quit when it's a little more calm."

"Oh, and when exactly is this great calmness going

to descend?" I ask. Smoking helps with stress? Maybe I should start. No, Battle hates it.

"I don't know, but it'll be sometime soon, so just shut up about it! I know it's an addiction. I know it's bad for me. I Just Like Doing It! Someday I will want to stop, I know that. Trust me," she says, walking over to the window with cigarette already in mouth.

"Do you have a lot of friends at home who smoke?" Battle asks suspiciously.

"No. But Mom does. She was mad when she found out I was, but she's kind of tolerating it now."

"How did you start?" I ask.

Katrina takes a reflective puff before she answers, and blows the smoke out the window. "I took one of hers out of her purse. I was all upset—it was around the time of the divorce—and Mom would always say that cigarettes were the only thing that kept her sane. I thought maybe if I had one, it would keep me sane too. It didn't, but I liked it anyway. Then I just started buying them and keeping them in my locker at school."

"So I guess they don't have locker searches where you are," I say.

"Nope. It's not that big a school, and everybody knows who smokes, even though you're not supposed to on campus."

"You're not supposed to here, either," Battle points out. Her voice sounds odd because she's holding her nose again.

"Yeah, and you see how much that gets enforced," Katrina says, exhaling a careful smoke ring. "Besides, how cool is that?" She gestures at the ring as it slowly disappears. "It took me forever to learn how."

"I always liked that in *Lord of the Rings*. It made me wonder if Tolkien knew how to blow smoke rings himself," I say.

"Oh, he must've. All those guys probably smoked like damn chimneys," says Battle.

"And drugs! Don't forget drugs! Opium and laudanum and . . . uh . . . other stuff that ends in 'um'! They did it all, I bet you anything!" says Katrina. Then she takes an extra long drag on her cigarette and produces another, larger, smoke ring.

"I can't picture the man who created Bilbo Baggins in an opium den," I say. "How about you guys?"

"Can I picture Tolkien in an opium den? Absolutely! He was a writer! If you're a writer you want to have as many kinds of experiences as you possibly can." Katrina finishes her cigarette and drops it into a Coke can on the windowsill, where it hisses briefly. "There, Battle, are you happy?"

"Not until you quit."

"Actually I meant, have you guys done drugs?" I feel naïve asking this, but I don't care, I'm curious.

"Not since we moved. I can't find anyone who sells out in the provinces. But on the plus side, it's easier to get liquor." Katrina gives a thumbs-up sign.

"Smoking anything is *vile*," says Battle with a glare at Katrina. "I've been in the same room with stoned people, but only at cast parties. How about you?" Battle turns to me.

Battle's lack of hair makes her eyes stand out even more. Beautiful Eyes Girl.

No. Just beautiful. "Cast parties for me, too," I say, trying not to look too much into Battle's eyes.

"Why do you ask, Nic? Are you jonesing? I don't have anything, but I bet we could find someone who does. Kevin must have some, don't you think he'd have some? We could call him, do you want to call him?" Katrina makes game show hostess gestures at the phone next to her computer.

"Don't call Kevin, he's got a test tomorrow," says Battle. Wait, how does she know?

I've never actually been stoned, just in the same room with it like Battle. I don't know if it works like alcohol and makes you say things you wouldn't normally say, but I bet it does. That would be a really bad idea for me right now.

"Oh, he wouldn't care, don't you think he wouldn't care?"

I scan the room and finally spot the little digital clock,

which is partially obscured by an orange tulle ballerina skirt. The glowing blue numbers read one-thirty A.M. I point at it and shake my head. "Volleyball," I say.

Battle nods and says, "We should get some sleep."

Katrina sighs. "You guys just do not understand the concept of decadence. At all."

July 4, 9:30 a.m., Volleyball Courts

I dreamed last night that I was defending Battle from her mom, using her braid as a weapon. How obvious can you get? Paging Dr. Freud.

You would think if I was going to dream about the person I'm infatuated with, I could at the very least manage to dream about kissing her. But if I did, I don't remember it.

Despite that, I'm in an oddly good mood—I feel exuberant and Katrina-esque. Maybe it's because the sun is shining and the sky is a particularly vivid blue. Or maybe the sugar and caffeine from last night haven't worn off yet.

I'm the first one of our group to get to the volleyball courts, which doesn't surprise me. I get a ball, stake out a space for us on a corner court—less chance of hitting other people that way—and wait. Pretty soon, Isaac shows up.

"How are you doing?" I ask, and bounce the ball over to him.

"Well, you know," he says, dribbling the ball loudly, "I tried slitting my wrists last night but it just doesn't work too well when all you've got is a spork."

"Ha ha—how are you really?"

He bounces the ball back to me. It slips out of my hands and I have to chase after it.

"You catch like a girl," he says.

"Yeah, well, you answer questions like a boy."

"I'm all right." After a minute, he adds, in a sing-song fake hick voice, "Thanks-fer-askin!" I shake my head.

The next person to arrive is Battle. My heart speeds up, right on schedule. I wonder if crushes are aerobic.

She looks mad—or is she just tired? I can't tell. Did Katrina say something to her about me after I went back to my room last night? I thought she left right after I did.

"It should be girls against boys," she says. "Don't you think that's best?"

"Holy shit, what happened to you?" asks Isaac.

I forgot—no one besides me and Katrina knows about her hair. Or rather, lack thereof.

"Like it?" She turns around, so Isaac can see that there is truly no hair whatsoever anywhere on her head.

"There's no *it* to like! Jesus! Why?" Isaac is clearly bewildered.

Battle shrugs.

"Man." He shakes his head. "I will *never* understand girls."

"Dude!" says Kevin. "Awesome! Can I feel your head?" He and Katrina both showed up without my noticing.

Battle lets him, smiling.

"Hey," he says after a minute. "Dude, with no hair you are gonna get *seriously* burned if you don't put on some sunscreen. Want some of mine?" He takes a tube out of one of the many pockets in his shorts and hands it to her. "Want me to do it?" he asks.

I realize that I am holding my breath.

Battle shakes her head and applies the sunscreen herself. "Thanks," she says, and hands the tube back to Kevin. I let out my breath, hoping it won't sound too loud. "Anyone else want some?" asks Kevin. Oh, so he's Mr. Health-Conscious now. Protect us from the evil ultraviolet rays, O Wise One.

"Nah, I want my skin to turn to beef jerky," says Isaac.

"No thanks," I force myself to say politely.

"I'll take some! My delicate complexion suffers so in this heat. And hey, for the game, I'll just be the cheerleader, okay?" says Katrina, taking Kevin's sunscreen and slathering most of the rest of it over her face and arms. "It'll still be good exercise; I'll jump up and down a lot."

"Somehow I doubt the RAs will go for it," Isaac says.

"How is this supposed to work again?" I ask. "It's been

a while since the last time it was forced on me. I know somebody serves the ball and then the other team tries to spike it, but that's all I remember."

"Is there love in this game?" asks Battle, running her hands distractedly across the top of her head as though she's not quite sure it is actually associated with the rest of her body.

"What the hell are you talking about?" asks Isaac.

"Love, you know, like in tennis! Love meaning zero," she explains.

"I always thought that was depressing," I say. "Why do they have to call it that?"

"Because they're realists," says Isaac. "They understand the true value of love," he continues, giving me a significant look.

Suddenly, I'm completely convinced that Isaac must know, too. I have no idea how he figured it out, but I'm sure he knows.

"Oh, that must be it," I say to cover my shock. Does everyone in the world know? Does *Kevin* know? God, I hope not.

"Hey, girls. You get on that side of the net. Isaac, come on over here to my side. First thing, we have to volley for the serve," says Kevin.

"Say that again in English," says Katrina.

"I hit the ball over the net. You guys hit it back. We hit

it back and forth until it hits the ground on somebody's side, and whoever's side that was, doesn't get to serve."

"If it hits the ground on their side, that hardly seems fair," I say.

"It's not supposed to hit the ground," Battle stage whispers.

"Oh!" I say. "You didn't tell me there was so much to keep track of. I should have brought my notebook."

"Watch some of the games around us for a while," Kevin says. "You'll figure out how it works."

We spend a few minutes scanning the other courts. There's one group that makes the game look like a complicated dance, the ball spinning in the air as it is launched from one side to the other. But the rest of the groups are composed of people who look as pathetic as I'm sure we're going to.

Kevin serves. Then Katrina hits the ball back, looking surprised and delighted that she has actually made contact with it. Isaac gets up close to the net and slams the ball back over, and I manage to get under it and hit it up into the air, and then Battle slams it over again and Kevin just misses getting it before it hits the ground.

"Good try!" an RA who's walking around from court to court says in an overly cheery way.

God. What kind of person would you have to be to *want* to be an RA?

"Your serve," Kevin says, and tosses the ball back to us. I catch it, and offer it to my teammates.

"Oh, god, don't make me do it—I've lost all sensation in my fingers," says Katrina.

"I'll do it," Battle says. I give her the ball, and she sends it spinning into the air with the exact right amount of force to land out of reach of both Isaac and Kevin, but still within bounds.

Aside from the whole gender question, Battle is beautiful and graceful and coordinated, and that just confirms that there's no hope for me. Maybe I can talk myself into a crush on Isaac after all. Of course I'd have to talk him *out* of his crush on Katrina, first.

I pretend I'm an anthropologist observing a ritual. "The tall boy (Kevin) exhibits a certain amount of skill," I imagine writing, "whereas his companion seems to be playing some sort of trickster-fool role." By which I mean that Isaac is a nutcase. He isn't very good, and he makes up for it by making a huge deal out of anything he does that shows any amount of skill whatsoever.

"Yes! I *will* take the Nike endorsements!" he yells into an imaginary phone.

He does little victory dances whenever he manages to spike the ball. They involve a lot of butt-wiggling. Sometimes we get to score because he's still doing his little victory dance when the ball comes back over onto his side of the net. Once, Battle actually manages to bounce the ball off his butt.

Katrina's strategy consists of jumping up and down a lot and yelling out sports-related terms completely at random.

"Double dribble!"

"Offsides!"

"Traveling!"

"High-sticking!"

She rarely makes contact with the ball, but when she does, she hits it more or less competently.

Battle plays with a certain lack of precision. For every time that she spikes the ball beautifully, there's a time when her very strong serve goes into somebody else's court and has to be retrieved, with copious apologies.

We realize after we've been playing for quite a while that we have absolutely no idea what the score is.

"That means we win!" yells Isaac.

"No, that means *we* win!" counters Katrina.

"Whoever scores the next point wins," says Kevin slowly and mildly.

After a few more minutes, Isaac misses the ball that Katrina has sent over the net, and immediately begins to claim that he missed it on purpose as a gentlemanly courtesy to us.

"Bullshit! Girls kick ass! And take names!" says Katrina, doing her own version of Isaac's butt-wiggling dance.

Battle retrieves the ball and says, "I'll take this back to the RA." Kevin follows her, which makes my stomach twist itself into a knot.

As soon as she's out of earshot, I say in a low voice, "Isaac, are you doing anything right now?"

"Other than regretting our tragic loss? No."

"I need to talk to you. Can we go for a walk?"

"Uh . . . sure. Now?"

I nod. "See you later," I say to Katrina, and start walking off the courts in the direction of the river, looking at the ground. I hope Isaac is following me. I hope Katrina doesn't think I'm trying to come onto him. No, she knows how I feel about Battle. She and the rest of the world.

"I think you know this already," I say. "I don't know what I think you can do about it, but I want to talk about it anyway."

He must think I have entirely lost my mind.

"I'm assuming this doesn't have anything to do with volleyball," Isaac says cautiously.

"Score one for you," I say. "Want to guess what it *does* have to do with?"

"I have no idea." He actually sounds like he doesn't.

A butterfly appears in the sky in front of me, a flickering

pattern of purple and pale yellow. I don't want to do anything but watch it, but it only stays near for a few moments, and then flutters away.

"Isaac, I—" My courage fails me. "I'm just really worried about you."

He looks at me as though I'm a bug that's just landed on his candy bar.

I shrug. The essential Isaac gesture. "You know. The whole thing with your parents."

I wish there were a rock handy that I could kick.

"I'm all right," he says.

Don't be all right. Please. Get upset, get mad, get something.

Awkward silence. Isaac shoves his hands in his pockets.

"Katrina thought you missed the wastebasket because you wanted us to know," I blurt.

"She did?"

"Yeah. That it was, you know, subconscious, but that you wanted us to find it, the letter, I mean."

"Jesus." Isaac shakes his head.

"You're not mad, are you?"

"It's a little late for that. You already know."

"I'm sorry."

We're at the river. I kick off my sandals, sit down, and put my feet in the water. It's cold, but it makes my ankle feel better. It only gets sore now when I walk for a long time.

Isaac leans against a weeping willow. "Is this really what you wanted to talk about?"

I kick my left foot up, splashing myself. "Yes!" I let it fall back into the water.

"So? What do you want to know?" He sounds angry now. So do I.

"Just, how *was* it, dealing with them? I mean, they came together, wasn't that weird? And how's your sister? Have you talked to her? Your mom said she was having a rough time, what does that mean?"

I'm slightly surprised to realize that I really want to know the answers to all these questions.

"I talked to her last night," he says, pulling a branch off the tree. "Rebecca—she's like Katrina. Anything that's up with her, you know it. Instantly. I think they thought if they brought her she'd cause a big scene and embarrass them in front of all the other parents." He begins ripping the leaves off the branch. Isaac is destructive to the natural world.

"Like, what kind of scene? What would she do?"

"Well, her big plan now is that we should get a place by ourselves, and just not even bother with Mom and Dad. She probably would've explained that to everyone at brunch."

"How old is she again?"

"Ten." He sits down next to me. "I'm not worried about her. She really digs Aunt Mim and Laura."

"Laura?"

"Yeah, she's my aunt's girlfriend."

"Girlfriend?" I squeak before I can stop myself.

Isaac thwacks the leafless branch lightly on the surface of the water. "Yep, that's right! My aunt's a big old dyke! Does that *bother* you?"

I start laughing, the crazy kind of laughing that isn't far from crying. "No," I finally manage to gasp. "And I bet it wouldn't bother you if I said I thought I might be one, too!"

"Really? Huh." Isaac sounds as though I'd just said I thought it looked like rain.

My surprise at his lack of reaction must show on my face, because he says, "Nic, remember, I'm from San Francisco. I assume everyone I meet is a bisexual pagan until proven otherwise."

All my muscles turn from wire to Jell-O with relief.

"It's because of Battle," I say before I lose my nerve again. "That's what makes me think it, that I might be."

I'll tell him everything. I'll make him admit he wants Katrina.

I wonder how old his aunt was when she knew.

It's raining, and it's very hot, and I feel like an entire pantheon is trying to hammer its way out of my head.

I can hear the rain splat against the sides of the building. Through the tiny windows of this room, I can see it falling: fat, heavy drops of rain that don't do anything but make it seem even hotter, as though the sky was sweating.

"Nic?" Anne pokes me. "Wake up."

"I wasn't asleep, just thinking."

"Well, your eyes were closed," Anne says.

"It's too hot to keep them open."

Anne looks perfectly cool and collected, as usual. No sweat has gathered on the keyboard of her laptop, though she's been taking notes as rapidly and conscientiously as always.

"Are you okay? You look kind of flushed." Anne's looking at me all concerned, as though I'm a potsherd she can't identify.

"I kind of have a headache," I admit.

"What do you want? I've got aspirin, ibuprofen, Midol . . ."

Of course she does. She probably keeps them in color-coordinated vials.

"Midol would be great, thanks."

She opens her purse, removes a tiny blue vial—I was right—shakes out two tablets, and gives them to me. She's probably got some fancy bottled water in her purse, too, but I decide not to push my luck. I swallow the tablets dry.

I just pray that Alex doesn't break in with one of his totally off-topic rants—I couldn't take his voice right now.

"But don't you think there's a responsibility to the greater society that's more valid than whether the bones happen to belong to some distant relative of some Indians?"

It's not Alex. It's his partner in crime, Ben, who likes to think that he's being hip and cynical when he's actually just being stupid and offensive. But at least Ben's voice doesn't grate on me the way Alex's does.

"What sort of responsibility are you referring to?" asks Ms. Fraser.

"The record of the past should belong to everybody. Catering to one group over another doesn't make sense," Ben says, putting his feet up on a desk.

"Anyone have another opinion?" Ms. Fraser asks.

I raise my hand. My headache is getting worse by the second, but I can't let him get away with that. I say, "So Ben, what you're saying is that you're really interested in the culture of the *ancestors* of Native Americans, but you couldn't care less about what the actual Native Americans who are living *now* think about the burials of their relatives being desecrated. That doesn't make sense to me, I don't know about anybody else."

Anne snickers.

Ms. Fraser clears her throat. "Thanks, you two. Ben's and Nicola's comments provide a good basic overview of the debate around these issues. There aren't any easy answers. Ben, I'm sure you can imagine a situation where you plan to excavate a site and the arguments of the indigenous people make you reconsider your plans. And Nicola, perhaps one day you'll be doing research on important human remains in a museum somewhere, only to find out that a tribe has demanded their return before you can finish your work."

I look back at Ben, who has wrinkled up his nose as though he smells something bad. I have an urge to stick my tongue out at him but decide that the action would be overly juvenile. Instead I merely wrinkle my nose in the same way and turn again to the front of the classroom to try and pay attention to Ms. Fraser.

My headache hasn't gotten any better. Headaches have been part of my personal cornucopia of PMS symptoms for years, but this one is much worse than normal. It must be stress.

I tried to eat dinner after class, but just the smell of the cafeteria made me gag. Battle made me drink juice so I'd get vitamin C, but that didn't help. I went to my room, turned off the lights, and pulled down the shades, but that didn't help either.

I paw through the shoebox of CDs that I brought with me and find *Carmina Burana*. It's not the most soothing piece of music in the world, but I love it so much, I think maybe hearing it will make me feel better. Or at least my head may start to throb in time with the percussion. I put the CD into my little boom box and lie back down.

As usual, while I listen, I stare at the picture on the CD cover—a medieval engraving of Fortune's wheel. Fortune's wheel has fascinated me since the first time Dad explained it to me—the idea that at any moment, the wheel could turn and a queen could become a peasant, or vice versa.

There's a knock at my door. When I sit up, my head spins, and when I stand up to walk to the door, I feel like I'm on some alien planet where I'm not used to the gravity.

"Um, hi—I thought you might still not be feeling well," says Battle. "I brought aspirin—and this." She holds out a washcloth full of something, with a rubber band around it, I guess to keep the something from spilling. "It's crushed ice. You, uh, put it on your head."

"Thank you," I manage to say, aware that I'm speaking more slowly and softly than usual. "Please come in, I kind of have to lie down again but don't—I mean, you don't have to leave."

Battle steps into my room and shuts the door quietly as

I collapse back onto the bed. Now my headache is mixed with the manic nervousness I get right before a concert or a show.

Carmina is suddenly loud, startling Battle. "What are you listening to?"

I point to the CD case, which I have conveniently left on the floor. She picks it up. "Oh—I know this. They choreographed part of it for us to do at All-State. Um . . . you have a headache?"

"I know," I say, louder than before, to be heard over the chorus that's blasting out of my boom box. "But I love it. I thought it might help."

Battle's still holding the washcloth full of ice. "Do you want this? You don't have to—"

"Oh, yes, I do," I say.

Battle walks to the bed, leans over, and very carefully places the ice-filled washcloth onto my forehead. There's a small trickle of sweat running down into the hollow of her neck, and her green tank top is clinging to her. I feel something start thudding more than my headache and realize it's my pulse. I hear her breathing, and mine, and then her face is so close and I lift my head just a little and our lips touch.

I close my eyes.

I am kissing her, and she is kissing me back.

I can still feel my head throb but the pain is very far away.

Even farther away, I hear the soprano solo. "Dulcissime," she sings, "totam tibi subdo me." Sweetest one, I give myself to you totally.

July 10, 9:30 p.m., My Room

field notes:

let's discuss this matter clinically. Kissing is wetter and softer than i with my romance novel education had expected and not quite as exciting except in retrospect. well, no, actually it is—i can't explain it any better than that. "frenching" (i hate that word) does live up to my expectations. that is really as "far" as we have gone.

what i am really afraid of is the next logical step in this process—i want to stay where we are now for a while at least. of course, looming in the distance is the perennial concern which i'm not even going to think about until this has lasted much longer than it has and "things" have gone much further. we'll burn that bridge when we come to it.

people's reactions:

kevin: does not appear to have noticed that anything has changed between me and battle. i have

begun to refer to him as captain clueless. he keeps
wanting to feel battle's head. she keeps letting him,
and doesn't even seem mad about it. i find this
somewhat disturbing.

isaac: has been great, although he's totally jealous,
since he still hasn't done anything about his crush on
katrina. if anything, he's a little too excited about
having "dyke friends." i said i thought i was bisexual,
since i'd been interested in guys before, and he said,
"by and by, you'll be gay!"

[bisexual is a weird word. it sounds like you
have to buy sex. or it could be one of those one-
celled creatures that you study in biology. "today,
class, we will study the life cycle of the bisexual."
"oh, i thought those were extinct."]

katrina: i don't quite know what's going on with
her. sometimes, she seems totally fine. other times she
is mean and resentful and i don't know why. maybe
she feels left out?

i wish isaac would just make a move on her.
he can't seem to figure out how.

ways for isaac to approach k.:

-fake that he has another computer problem. make
sure to do it when no one else is around for her to
rope in.

-ask for advice about where he should live; she loves to give advice.

   -(unhealthy but could work) ask for a cigarette, have her teach him to smoke.

   -get a really bad headache (worked for me!)

   -just tell her he's interested (totally unlikely).

field notes:

   the whole idea of body language makes so much more sense to me now.

   when she's happy, battle can't stay still. she does these things with her arms that look almost like hula or a belly dancer, except she doesn't move her hips in the same way. she'll walk with a lilt in her stride. not a whole "i'm sexy" kind of strut (although she is)—it's just as though she's hearing this great music and is walking with the rhythm. it's like no one ever told her that being awkward was a possibility.

   and the funny thing is, when i see her move like that, instead of feeling like i'm this giant maladroit klutz who should really avoid doing anything involving physical coordination, i can ... i can sort of hear her music, too.

"This reminds me of the Indian Tree."

Battle looks up at me from the lower branch where she's sitting. "The Indian Tree?"

"It's this giant, dead tree—it's been dead for as long as I can remember. All the bark is stripped off so it's just smooth, like a piece of furniture. I used to climb it all the time with Jamie—I mean *James*."

"You said that name like it made you want to spit. An ex?"

"I don't have any exes. You're the—I mean, no. It's like this. When James was Jamie, when we were little, we were best friends. We made potions. We deciphered signs that only we knew were important. When we were nine, he moved away. I missed him so much that I saved up all this money for a whole summer so I could go find him. I went on the bus for hours by myself. When I got there, to his new house, he was already friends with all these boys, and he was James, and he was awful. The End."

"Ouch. What kind of signs?" Battle has to squint a little to look up at me since the sun is so bright this afternoon.

"Oh—like which way a branch was pointing would be the way we'd walk that day. And you know how when they're doing work on sewers or power lines or something, they paint little squiggle things on the road and the sidewalk? We'd come up with all these crazy meanings for them. That kind of thing."

"It sounds great. Sorry he turned out to be a jerk."

I'm dangling my legs down from my branch, and Battle touches my calf briefly in sympathy. It sends a shock from my leg all the way up my spine.

"Who was your best friend, growing up?" I ask, to regain my composure. I can't get used to this.

She sighs. "Nic."

"I'm sorry, is it an awful story? You don't have to—Oh. You mean Nick-with-a-K. Right?"

She nods. "We were just a really close family. Until we stopped."

"Anyone besides him?"

It's funny. Being here, up in the tree, sitting on different branches—it makes it easier to talk somehow. Is it because we can't look directly at each other?

Battle sighs again. "I'm shy, in case you hadn't noticed."

"I hadn't." How can she say she's shy? She's dated people. She's the one who kissed *me,* the first time.

"If Katrina hadn't made me come over the first day, I probably never would have talked to any of you." She has a finger in her mouth as she says this.

"But—you're so—" Beautiful. Brilliant. Amazing. "You seem so sure of yourself, the way you talk, just the way you *are*. I mean, you're not like Katrina—you don't talk a lot, but everything you say, it just feels . . . important."

Battle's finger is bleeding. "I don't talk a lot because words don't always work."

Yes, they do, I want to say, but I can't, for some reason. Which means she's right.

But I can't let the silence hang, either—I ask something that's been bothering me for a while.

"When he left, what did your parents do? I mean, did they try to find him?"

Battle says flatly, "They fought. Mom wanted to call the police, hire a private detective, the whole shebang. Dad said it was Nick's choice to leave, and he'd get in touch with us when he was ready."

"Who won?"

"No one."

It's another of her nonanswers. Doesn't she want me to know anything about her? I try another approach.

"It's so awful when parents fight. Mine almost divorced when I was nine. They didn't yell, they just got cold and overly polite—like suddenly we were all living in some strange hotel. Do your parents yell?"

"No."

All right, that didn't work either. Third time's the charm?

113

"Hey, this is totally off topic, but how long have you had Dante and Beatrice?"

Battle smiles up at me for the first time since we started talking about her brother.

"They came from the same litter—the mother belonged to one of the families from church. I got them . . . four years and thirty-seven days ago. They were eight weeks old. Mom and Dad weren't sure I'd be able to take care of them, but I read every book in the library about dogs and took lots of notes. And I kept track of their growth. I measured them and weighed them every day—I paper-trained them and got them used to being on leashes—oh, I miss them!"

The ache in her voice makes me miss them, too, even though I've never seen them except in her pictures, and I've always hated dogs.

"Wow, you did all that? That's really impressive. You'd make a great vet," I say.

Battle looks so surprised it almost makes me laugh. "That's exactly what I want to be," she says softly.

July 14, 6:30 a.m., My Room

<u>field notes:</u>

last night when i was coming out of battle's room, this girl i don't know looked at me like i was a three-headed monster, and absolutely scuttled away from me down the hall like she thought i was going to breathe fire or something.

but on the other side, the angst crow who was so mean to me when i liked her dress saw battle and me walking around holding hands and she actually smiled—although she turned it into a scowl as soon as she saw that i had noticed.

alex and ben from class also look at me like i'm a three-headed monster, but then i look at them the same way, and have since day one.

i've started to keep track of the number of times i hear someone mutter the word "dyke" in my direction—five so far.

i guess i should be getting angry, or upset, but more than anything it's just odd—what has changed about me, that makes these people now want to call me this name? do i look different? it's not as though battle and i have been out necking constantly. not that i'd mind. or would i? i don't know—whenever we're outside, in public, something happens that keeps us from doing anything but holding hands. like magnets that repel each other if they get too close.

i've also been wondering if it's a new phenomenon for there to be tons of [boy/girl] couples all over the place, practically having sex on the lawn, or if they've been there all term and i'm only just now noticing.

i've tried to look for other (ahem) same-sex couples, too, but it's hard to tell. so many girls are all over each other, holding hands or doing each other's hair or giving each other back rubs. it's impossible to know if you're looking at friendship or lust.

or both.

as for boys . . . there are some jocky-looking guys who are forever punching each other on the arm or slapping each other on the butt. i suppose it's possible they could have something going on, but you'd certainly never catch them, say, kissing.

and there's another boy i've seen, i think he's in katrina's class, who often wears long velvet skirts and lots of black eyeliner. but i believe this to be a fashion statement rather than a declaration of sexuality, since i have observed him making out with various angst crows.

i suppose he could like boys, too, though.
i of all people should remember that.

July 15 (one-week anniversary), 6:30 a.m., My Room

<u>field notes:</u>
battle noticed my viola last night. "how long have you been playing?"

i told her—since i was in fifth grade—and she said, "that's how long i've been dancing. play something for me."

"only if you dance," i said, expecting her to laugh and change the subject.

"all right," she said.

so i opened my case and took out my bow to put rosin on it, something i always do when i'm especially nervous about playing.

it didn't need any rosin, but it gave me something to do for a minute while i tried to figure out what i knew well enough to play from memory while i watched her dance.

finally i remembered a little bach piece i did years ago for the solo-ensemble festival. "this is slow," i said. "i hope you didn't want something fast."

battle shook her head.

the way she was standing, it's as though her whole body was listening. which i suppose it was.

the strings were remarkably easy to tune. no doubt this was because the rain the other day reduced the amount of humidity in the air, but i prefer to attribute it to the intervention of some patron spirit of music and dance.

i closed my eyes and ran through the first few bars in my head before i put the viola on my shoulder.

i don't know how well i was playing, but my viola was in very good voice.

violas in good voice sound like expensive dark chocolate tastes, rich and swirling and complex.

and that's the kind of moves she made, all loose arms and light, long legs, and i knew, just for a minute, what music was for.

July 16, 7:30 a.m., Outside Katrina's Room

Battle and I have been knocking on Katrina's door for what seems like hours before she finally stumbles loudly across her room and opens it. "Well, if it isn't my two favorite lesbians," she says groggily. "Siddown while I get dressed."

"I don't know if that word fits," I say. "Do you think we're lesbians, Battle?"

Battle doesn't say anything. Katrina says, pulling a violently orange T-shirt out of her cardboard clothes box, "What the hell else would you be? Unless you'd prefer the word . . . oh, god, I can't remember, it was in this weird old movie I saw . . . inverts, that was it."

"It sounds like we'd have to stand on our heads all the time," I say.

Battle promptly puts her hands on the floor and kicks her legs up into a beautiful headstand. I grab her ankles and hold her up, both of us giggling. "Wow, I can do this so much better now that I don't have hair to get in my face!" she says. Fortunately—unfortunately?—her tank top is tight enough that it doesn't ride up.

"Seriously though, what's wrong with being lesbians?" Katrina zips up her jeans.

"I don't think there's anything wrong with it," I say, holding Battle's ankles as she walks a few steps on her hands, "I'm just not sure it describes us completely accurately. I mean, I've liked boys before. And Battle, didn't you say that you had dated boys?" I turn my head sideways and peer down at her face, which is getting flushed. She nods.

Katrina says, "But wouldn't that just be because you

hadn't found a girl yet who was, you know, willing? I mean, it seems like it's a lot easier to find boys than it would be to find girls—not that I'm looking for a girl, mind you. And come on, Nic, Battle lives in the South. Ho-mo-sex-shuality is probably still, like, illegal there, right?"

Battle shakes her head. "No."

"Yeah, but your dad's a minister! Wouldn't he shit bricks?" asks Katrina. "Come to think of it . . . aren't they going to be really mad about the whole shaving your head thing, let alone what's going on with you and Nic? They just didn't look like free-expression types to me."

Battle shakes her legs free of my hands, comes out of the headstand and stands up. "Breakfast is almost over," she says. "Are you ready?"

July 17, 11:39 p.m., Battle's Room

This is a different kind of shy than I've ever felt before. Being shy was always about not knowing what to say to people, being afraid I'd say something stupid that would make them laugh at me.

Now—now it's about not knowing what to do. If I sit on the bed, is that too forward, like I'm expecting that we'll immediately start making out? If she wants a back rub, is it too much to kiss the back of her neck?

I'm sitting on the floor trying to do the reading for class tomorrow, and Battle's sitting next to me. She's finished her work for the evening, so she's rereading this incredibly battered copy of *All Creatures Great and Small*.

"Your hair's all tangled," Battle says suddenly. She gets up, walks to her dresser and retrieves a large wooden brush. It still has some blonde hairs entwined in its bristles.

She sits directly behind me and brushes my hair with just the right amount of pressure, not so tentative that I can't feel it or so hard that my scalp gets sore.

"That's so nice," I say, and my voice comes out deeper than I mean it to, almost in a purr.

"I've had a lot of practice."

"I guess you must have; your hair was longer than mine's ever been," I say.

"There's that—but also I brush Dante and Beatrice a lot." She snickers.

I attempt to bark.

"Silly," says Battle, putting down the brush and leaning in to kiss me.

Now I understand why so many songs talk about desire as electric.

If I could harness what I'm feeling now, I could power a city.

———

i want to make battle a present. maybe for our three-week anniversary? the dog book was good, but i want her to have something that i've actually created.

but what?

a drawing? no, i suck.

i'll keep thinking about this.

July 18, 7:45 p.m., Underneath the Big Tree in the Courtyard

Battle and I are working on our respective homework. In my case this means a haphazard pile of xeroxed articles and notes with drawings in the margins; in hers it means a neat stack of books with post-it notes marking relevant passages.

This is the first day in the past several that hasn't been incredibly hot. The sky is a mix of pink and lavender, fading into blues and grays, and there's the slightest bit of a breeze blowing.

"I've been looking for you everywhere! I assumed you were enjoying each other's favors in some secluded corner," says Katrina.

"That *is* what we're doing. These articles are all actually from the Kama Sutra," I say.

"It is imperative that you come to my room immediately," Katrina continues, ignoring me. "We Must Talk." I can hear the capital letters.

"Why can't we talk here?" I ask.

Katrina ducks behind the tree and sticks her head out at an angle. "Spies," she says in a stage whisper. "They're everywhere! Plus that's where all the caffeine is. And the rest of my cigarettes—I'm almost out!"

"Oh, horrors," says Battle. "You mean you might have to live without your daily dose of toxins?"

"Shut up. Come on!" Katrina is jumping up and down.

We get up, too slowly for Katrina, and follow her inside and up the stairs to her room.

Battle's hair has already started to grow back. I thought it would be a prickly stubble, like when you shave your legs. But it's more like suede, and even as short as it is, it still catches the light and gives her a halo.

"All right, so here's the thing," Katrina says, falling backwards into her beanbag chair. "You may think this is kind of weird. But hey—you guys are all deviant and sinning, at least according to my grandparents you would be, so you don't have any excuse to be shocked."

"I'm so glad we can be a *National Enquirer* article for you," I say as I stroke the fuzz on top of Battle's head.

Battle asks, "What deviant thing are you doing?"

Katrina lights a cigarette and inhales deeply. "Nothing—yet. But I just have this feeling. I really think it's not just me."

She's finally come to her senses! I want to call Isaac.

"Yeah," she continues, "the way he's been acting in class, just the way he looks at me, how he asks me questions sometimes, the things he writes on my assignments . . ."

Wait, Isaac doesn't have class with her.

"Katrina, are you talking about your *teacher?*" I ask. *Teacher* comes out as a shriek.

"Of course—why do you think I said *deviant?*"

Battle's shaking her head. Through her held nose, she intones, "*Beyond* bad plan. Do you want to get kicked out? Besides, I've seen that Carl of yours, and he looks like a damn toad." She leans her head on my shoulder. I take her hand.

For a split second, Katrina grins, but then she is all righteous indignation. "Carl is very *distinguished* looking, and he has a *brilliant* mind."

"Jesus, Katrina," I say, coughing. "Would you blow that out the window?—sorry, Battle," I add, since I dislodged her head when I coughed.

I'm just so angry and sad, suddenly. I hadn't realized how much I was rooting for Isaac. Obligingly, Katrina gets up, perches on the windowsill, and blows her smoke outside.

I pick up one of Katrina's red plastic lizards and test

how far its tail will bend. Then I start whacking myself on the leg with it. Battle gives me a weird look.

"Promise me," I say, "that you won't make some Lolita move on him."

"Excuse me—" Katrina stubs her cigarette out on the windowsill and tosses the butt—"I thought I was asking for some support from my girls."

"This *is* support," says Battle. "Support means not letting your friends do stupid things." She takes the plastic lizard away and then holds out her hand to me, apparently as a substitute. I take it.

It takes about an hour to talk Katrina down, and even then, I'm not convinced that we've actually made a lasting impression.

I understand about brain lust. I know what it's like when you hear someone's voice and, no matter what they're saying, you want to sit and listen for the rest of your life. I even understand getting a crush on a teacher—it's like an extreme version of the teacher's pet scenario, which most of us with more than a few brain cells to rub together have experienced. But thinking, even expecting, that the teacher is going to *respond* . . . not good.

"I don't get what this whole teacher crush thing is about. I mean, didn't it seem to *you* like she was into Isaac?" I ask Battle as we walk back to her room.

"It's safe," says Battle quietly.

"But why would Katrina worry about being *safe?* She's had *cyber*sex! She wears leggings that say 'Fuck' on them! She's the most flamboyant person I've ever *met!*"

"Exactly," says Battle, unlocking her door.

"Exactly what?"

"Everyone wants to be safe."

"Oh. I *think* I see what you mean," I say, even though I don't, really. Because we're about to go inside her room. Which means that we'll probably not be talking for much longer.

We've been doing this for the past several nights. She'll go to my room or I'll come to hers, "things" will happen until one of us mumbles something about a paper, or reading, that we really have to do, and then whichever of us whose room it isn't will leave. I don't know what to think about this. I always thought that if you were *with* someone, you'd talk about it: what it meant, things that scared you, something. Battle's right: words *don't* always work.

You'd never know that around my house, though. Even when Mom and Dad are fighting, they never resort to the silent treatment. They just speak in precise, overly enunciated voices. In fact, their words get *longer.* How was I supposed to learn to deal with someone who doesn't want to talk at all?

I've been doing a lot of drawing: goofy, dreamy little

sketches of her nose, her right foot, her hands—parts of her. I don't know what they add up to.

Battle holds her hand up to stop me from following her into her room. "Wait," she says. "I'll just be a minute."

Why?

I sit cross-legged outside her door, imagining insane, inane things. Is she putting on special lingerie, like in a romance novel? Did she actually make a mess for once in her life and has to clean it up before she'll let me in? What if—? The door opens, and she steps out, carrying a blanket and wearing jodhpurs instead of the shorts she had on before. Are jodhpurs romantic?

"Remember our hike?" she asks. "Your ankle's better, right?"

I nod. "It's past curfew," I say automatically.

"So?"

"Okay, sure."

Battle's walk looks peculiar, more cautious than usual. Both of us are cautious as we walk past the RA's closed door, as though it will suddenly pop open and our alleged chaperone will say, "J'accuse!" It doesn't, of course.

Battle is heading for the woods. I think about suggesting that we go to the river instead, but somehow, that's Isaac's and my place, and I want to keep it that way.

Sharp pine scent fills my nostrils, and the trees make it suddenly much darker, and we have to walk even more slowly. The needles are damp on the ground. I feel them on my toes, since I'm wearing sandals.

The woods are different at night. When I was very little I had this idea that there were day-trees and night-trees: two completely different species. The night-trees were dangerous, but more beautiful than the day-trees.

"Here," says Battle. We're in a tiny clearing. The tree stumps look like they would make perfect chairs, so I sit down on one. Immediately my butt gets wet and I feel foolish. Then I look up, and Battle is taking off her jodhpurs. "Yes! It worked!"

Oh my god. Am I supposed to strip now? *What* worked?

Battle's jodhpurs are at her ankles. She has carefully untied two scarves from around her right thigh. The scarves were securing something wrapped in a third scarf, which she hands to me before she pulls the jodhpurs back up.

I'm relieved, yet disappointed.

"Unwrap it," she says. My hands are a little shaky as I unwind the warm purple silk. I can't stop thinking about where this something has been during our walk into the woods. Then I see what it is, and start laughing at Battle's ingenuity.

"I was going to tie a loaf of bread to my other leg, but I ran out of scarves," she says.

"Just a bottle of wine and thou is perfect." I don't think I've ever been this happy. If I looked up, I could see the stars. But I'd rather look at Battle.

"How did you get it?" I can't believe Battle has wine.

"I brought it with me . . . in the one bag that Mom didn't stand over me while I was packing. It's left over from a cast party." She smirks.

"Wow. So you just randomly thought that you might want some wine while you were at the institute?" I ask, still holding the bottle.

"I thought this year would be different. I just didn't know how different." She smiles, a little nervously.

"Wow," I say. "Uh, so do you have a corkscrew?"

Battle looks stricken. "Oh hell. Give it here."

I hand her the bottle, and she scrutinizes the tinfoil that covers its top. Then, she rips the foil off decisively and announces with triumph,

"Twist-off!"

She sits down, twists off the cap, and takes a swig from the bottle.

"I'd forgotten how awful it is," she says with horrified delight. "Have some."

I say, "With a recommendation like that, how can I resist?"

She passes me the wine. I put my lips to the bottle's

mouth and tilt it back to drink. The wine rushes onto my tongue and down my throat faster than I thought it would, and I cough and sputter.

"Yuck! It tastes like rotten grapes!" I say, when I can talk again.

"Isn't that the point?" Battle asks, taking the bottle from me.

"I didn't think it was supposed to taste so *much* like rotten grapes," I say, while Battle takes another sip. When she's finished, she says, "Well you see, Ms. Lancaster, you simply have not educated your palate properly. If you had an educated palate, you would see—"

"That this is really vile!" I interrupt. "Give me more."

I take a larger gulp this time. As awful as the wine tastes, it's already making my insides buzz and my face flush in a way that I like. It reminds me of sometimes when I do line drawings and the lines are too harsh. I smudge the lines with the edge of my pinky, and they get softer and more blurry. That's what's happening to my brain.

I slide off the stump and onto the blanket next to Battle.

"Your face is so red. It's cute," says Battle. She reaches over and strokes my cheek.

"You're so beautiful," I say. She blushes.

"Don't lie," she says.

I grab her shoulders and stare into her face. "You are."

"You *have* been drinking!" she says.

I want to say "I love you," but I'm scared to.

So I kiss her instead. Then we have more wine.

The wine makes it easier. Everything we've been awkward about, all those steps we haven't taken yet, all of it gets blurry and soft until all that's left is sensations: cool night air on skin, hands and mouths moving over each other, the scent of pine mixed with lavender, the sound of breath.

"You were so beautiful, I had to draw you. But I didn't admit to myself what I was feeling until I was trying to write this thing for class, about you, and it was supposed to be objective and I just couldn't be—"

"You wrote about me?" She doesn't sound pleased, I realize dimly, but I'm full of love and wine, and my voice is running on,

"I didn't turn it in! Anyway, that was when I knew, and it just got more and more intense—like when I was cutting your hair, I can't believe I didn't stab you with the scissors, I was so nervous! When did you know? Was there a particular moment when you realized it? Were you worried? Were you happy? What made you decide to come to my room that night when I had the headache?"

"Why do you have to take everything apart?"

"So I can figure out how it fits together."

"What if it *breaks?* Don't talk. Shut up and feel."

———

"Come on, we have to get back." Battle's voice is abrupt.

I blink dazedly, my head beginning to throb. It's still dark—we haven't been out all night, anyway. I hope I haven't been snoring. My mouth tastes like something died inside it. Battle is standing impatiently over me. "What'd you do with the bottle?" I ask.

"Buried it. Come on!"

I stand up, feeling slow-witted and clumsy. She buried the bottle? I would have thought she wouldn't want to get her hands dirty. "Here," says Battle. "I forgot, I wanted to give this to you." She hands me the purple scarf. There's dirt underneath her fingernails.

I thought she was mad at me. Now I don't know what to think. I wind the scarf around my neck, liking the way it feels against my skin.

"Thank you," I say to the back of her head, and begin following her.

My head throbs, and so does my ankle. *Is* Battle mad at me? If she is, what for?

At the edge of the woods, Battle stops walking, and turns around to face me. I wait for her to say something, but she doesn't. Instead she puts her arms around me, hugs me so hard it almost hurts, and doesn't let go for a long time.

———

An RA catches us walking up the stairs to our floor.

"Do you remember the ground rule about curfew?" she asks.

We nod.

"You chose to break that rule, and I am going to have to write up a warning for each of you. Do you think you made a good choice?"

Yes, I think, remembering Battle's arms around me. *Yes, yes, yes.*

July 19, 7 p.m., Katrina's Room

"What do you need it for again?" Katrina asks, rummaging through her giant box of clothes.

"Something I'm making for Battle—I mean, if that's okay with you, if you can spare it."

"Oh, sure, raid my wardrobe for all your deviant needs. . . . What are you making, some kind of fabric-covered sexual aid?" Katrina holds up a pair of green velvet leggings. "Here, these don't really fit me, goddammit, so you can use them."

"They look perfect! Thanks a lot," I say.

"So, what are you making?"

"A present."

I can't be any more specific than that. If I told her it was a puppet, she'd want to know why the hell I was making one, and then I'd have to tell her about Nick-with-a-K, and then Battle would never speak to me again.

"A present," Katrina mimicks coyly. "God, you and Battle are rubbing off on each other—what kind of—"

"Yup, every chance we get!" I interrupt, cackling evilly. "Thanks again, see ya at breakfast!"

field notes:
—cut up the leggings to make dress
—hair will be her real hair, from the braid (duh)
need: sculpey for the head & hands, stuffing for body (where to get?), a crown

July 20, 12:30 p.m., Cafeteria

"I'm gonna write a song about your head," Kevin says to Battle. She laughs. Kevin rubbing Battle's head has become a daily lunchtime ritual, and every day it makes me more uncomfortable. Have I said anything about this to Battle? No, of course not. Why? Well—all together now—words don't always work.

Battle asks, sounding almost painfully interested, "You write songs, too?"

We all know he composes for orchestra, that's unavoidable. Sometimes he'll look up from the music he's always carrying, and just start going off about the influence of nineteenth-century popular music on symphonic structure, or how Alban Berg was a genius, or how five other composers I've never heard of were actually far more significant than Elvis and the Beatles.

Kevin nods. "You guys know Nietzsche, right?"

This question shocks me. Despite his nearly constant composing and his mentions of obscure musicians, I still think of Kevin as a moron. ("Cut him some slack," Katrina said once when I'd made it more clear than usual what an idiot I thought he was. "His first language isn't language.")

"That Which Does Not Kill Us Makes Us Stronger," says Isaac in an Arnold Schwarzenegger voice.

"I tell you you must learn to harbor chaos if you wish to give birth to a dancing star," says Kevin, apparently at random.

"Is that Nietzsche, too?" Battle asks.

"Yeah. It's where my band's name comes from: Chaos Harbor." Kevin takes a giant bite of brownie.

"That works," Katrina says.

"I don't know if it does," I say. "I mean, think about what a harbor is, and think about what chaos is. They cancel each other out. A harbor is all about things going into their proper places, like a safe harbor, you know? And

135

chaos is about nothing being where you think it's going to be at all."

"That's why it's so cool," says Kevin with his mouth full. "It's like, you have to make a space for all this chaos, so that's the harbor, but then you don't know what the chaos is going to do, and so that's the chaos."

"That's deep, man. You should have lived in the sixties," says Isaac, sounding nearly as disgusted as I am. Go, Isaac.

"Only if I could've jammed with Jimi," says Kevin.

"We could set your guitar on fire; that'd be almost as good," says Isaac.

Kevin shakes his head.

"How about if we just gave you a lot of drugs?" asks Katrina.

"That'd be cool," says Kevin.

"So, are you learning anything in Music Theory?" I ask. My voice sounds brittle.

"Nothing you'd understand. No offense, but it's all pretty technical. Schenkerian analysis, stuff like that."

I wish I had the faintest notion what Schenkerian analysis was.

"Is it helping you with your composing?" Battle asks. He nods vigorously.

"Definitely. It's way beyond the circle-of-fifths crap I had in school. I've gotten to a whole new level, I can tell."

"Oh, Mister Composer Sir, I hope one day I will be lucky enough to solo with your orchestra," says Isaac.

"Isaac! I didn't know you played an instrument! What do you play?" I ask.

Instead of answering in words, Isaac licks his left hand, sticks it underneath his right armpit, and starts making disgusting noises. Isaac is such a good friend that I had allowed myself to forget until now that he is a Teenage Boy™. Everyone is irritating me today.

"That's nothing. I bet you can't belch on command," says Katrina.

"Can you?" asks Isaac.

Katrina belches. Isaac and Kevin applaud.

I say, "You are all totally gross. I'm going to go read about nice inoffensive dead people and where they put their garbage and what that says about their culture."

"I bet they could *all* belch on command. I bet it was their most important religious ritual. And you could be studying the way it has come down to us today, but no, you're going to bury your head in some dry old book," says Isaac.

"If I find anything in the book about the Grand Exalted Burpfests of Sumeria, I'll be sure to let you know," I say, trying not to look at the way Battle is looking at Kevin.

———

When I knock on Battle's door, much later, she only opens it a little way. She says, "I've got a big test tomorrow that I have to study for—you should probably just stay in your room tonight."

I'm so stunned that it doesn't even occur to me to say that we've studied together before without any problem.

I walk back to my room and sit on my bed for a while, feeling dull and confused. Then I walk down the hall to Katrina's room. She opens it and says, "Geez, I never see you around this late. Did you and Battle run out of whipped cream or something?"

I explain what Battle said to me. Katrina says,

"Did you consider that maybe she has a big test tomorrow that she has to study for?"

"But I don't know why she didn't tell me about it before."

"Maybe she finds your presence just a teensy bit distracting, and she didn't remember to tell you before now?"

"Maybe," I say. "But I still don't understand."

"Well, then you should talk to her about it tomorrow. Assume that she really does need to study tonight, and don't bug her, but talk to her tomorrow," Katrina says. She sounds impatient.

"It's not fair," I say. "You're making way too much sense. I wanted to whine."

"You should always feel free to whine, hon, but it won't change my opinion," says Katrina. "And actually, no joke, I have a bunch of homework to get done tonight myself. I'm gearing up for my masterwork for Carl. And I'm in a really bad mood, because I am bleeding like the proverbial stuck pig. Hey, maybe *that's* why Battle doesn't want to see you."

"I hadn't thought about that. Mine hasn't started yet."

"Oh my god, Nic, maybe you're *pregnant!* Alert the media, it's the first lesbian conception without artificial insemination!" Katrina cackles.

I fold my arms across my chest. "Why are you so *obsessed* with the whole lesbian thing? I've liked boys before, I probably will again, so I believe that the appropriate word is *bisexual,* since you're so desperate to give me a label."

"Why are *you* so obsessed with *not* being one? I believe that that the appropriate word is *denial.*"

I sigh. I don't know what I am, I just want to see Battle, and getting angry at Katrina isn't going to help. "I'm sorry I bugged you, Katrina, I'll let you get back to your homework."

Katrina is instantly pure sympathy again. "Hey, no worries, bug me any time, even if I'm bitchy. 'Cause that's—what—friends—*are*—for," she sings tunelessly.

"Thanks."

I'm some kind of cosmic ingrate. They really *are* my

friends—better friends than I've ever had, better even than Jamie before he was James—and that's not enough anymore.

I walk back to my room slowly.

After I unlock my door, it suddenly occurs to me that I haven't picked up my viola since I played for Battle. I close my door, and then I kneel down in front of the bed as though I'm about to say my good-night prayers. I reach the case out from underneath my bed, unzip the cover, unfasten the latches, and open the lid. The blue velvet lining looks incongruous as usual, as though my viola is wearing an evening gown.

It takes forever to tune the damned thing. It's too humid.

I should warm up, do some scales or études. But I'm not practicing to practice—I'm practicing so I can make my mind do something other than obsess about why Battle sent me away.

There's a piece I always play when I'm depressed. It's a viola transcription of the slow movement of Tartini's *Devil's Trill* violin sonata. I can't play the fast movement to save my life, but the slow one is mostly about double stops, vibrato, and of course trills. Whenever Mom hears me start playing it, she'll knock on my door and ask if everything's okay.

Nobody's going to do that tonight.

I'm not a real musician, not like goddamn Kevin the

Brilliant Composer God. Chaos Harbor. Jesus Christ. I know the harbor he wants for *his* chaos.

Maybe she wants that, too.

Stop it. Play your damn viola.

Something happens, sometimes, when I play. The only way I can explain it is that I go further inside whatever I'm feeling, and the feeling itself doesn't seem to matter as much as what the feeling and the music are mixing together to make.

I tighten my bow and start rubbing rosin onto it. The repetitive motion is comforting. Then I fasten the little cloth covering back onto the rosin cake and put it back into my case.

I take my viola out and spend a few minutes messing with my shoulder rest, getting it into the right position. Then I pick up the bow again and put the viola under my chin.

It feels good to plant my fingertips on the thick strings. It hurts a little, too. My fingers have gotten soft. And some of my chords are dissonant in a way that Tartini never intended them to be.

Someone bangs angrily on the wall.

Oh, that's right. It's late.

But I don't feel considerate, so I play until my fingers are sore and my neck is tired. Then I put my viola away and start working on the puppet.

"Okay, I have something for you—I really hope you like it, I made it myself, although I did use something of yours—"

"What is it, a voodoo doll?" Battle sounds amused.

"No! If it was a voodoo doll, I wouldn't be giving it to you, I'd be using it to make you obey my every whim! But I figure I can persuade you most of the time to do what I want anyway. . . ."

"Ha!" says Battle, pulling my hair. We kiss.

Then I pull away. "You're distracting me when I'm trying to give you a present!"

"Oh, excuse me." Battle gets up and sits on the other side of the room.

I take a deep breath and say, "All right, so after you showed me the puppet that was Nick-with-a-K's, I couldn't stop thinking about it, and everything you said about how you guys used to do puppet shows together, and I just thought, why doesn't she have her own? I mean, obviously that one was Nick's, so where's Battle's?"

Battle is frowning, but mostly that just means she's listening intently.

"And then it hit me: of course you wouldn't have it, because Nick would have taken it with him when he left. As kind of a reminder of you, a way he could take you with him, even though he was leaving you behind. And the more I thought about that, the more I thought: I want to make her a new one. I know it's not like having Nick-with-a-K back, but it was just something I wanted to do for you, just, you know, because, and anyway, here it is. She is, I, um, call her the Empress. Empress of the World."

I walk across the room and put the Empress into Battle's hands. She came out really well, I think: the green velvet leggings made a beautiful dress, the head and hands actually don't look mutated, and Battle's hair is so gorgeous that there's no way it could look anything but great. Of course, I didn't braid it.

Battle is turning the Empress around in her hands, which are shaking a little, I notice. Wow, I didn't think she'd be so excited. I feel a warm glow of accomplishment.

Then I notice that her shoulders are shaking, too.

"Stop—stop trying to *explain* me. I can't take this," Battle says through tears.

She holds the Empress out to me. "Please go," she says.

"Battle, I'm so sorry. I didn't know it would upset you, I don't under—"

"*Please.*"

I go.

Part Two

<u>field notes:</u>
things to forget:
   ~~incredible clear green eyes~~
   ~~the way she moves~~
   ~~her slight sweet drawl~~
   ~~lavender~~
   EVERYTHING.

147

"Explain this to me again. Why aren't you and Battle speaking to each other?"

"She didn't like a present I made for her," I say helplessly.

"The one you used my leggings for? The one that for some reason, you won't actually explain to me what it is? Was it some weird sex thing? And then she wasn't into it, and she got mad?"

I shake my head. It suddenly occurs to me that when Katrina doesn't know what's going on, she makes up a story to make all the things she doesn't understand make sense.

And that I do the same thing.

And that Battle doesn't. Ever.

field notes:

when you play the viola a lot, you get a red mark on your neck that looks not unlike a hickey. this causes people like isaac to make lewd comments, until they remember. then they feel all sheepish, and you have to tell them it's okay, even though it isn't.

July 25, 4:42 p.m.,
Under the Big Tree in the Courtyard

"This is the nastiest assignment I have ever had in my life," I say. I have rubber gloves on. Ms. Fraser passed them out in class a few days ago. She said, "I don't know why, but parents just seem to worry when you tell them that their children need to buy rubber gloves for one of their assignments."

I am sifting through the contents of a medium-sized plastic Ziploc bag. I have ten of these bags. They contain samples from the contents of several different garbage cans, picked (by me) from different buildings around campus. Some of them are the kind of garbage cans that are just for cigarettes, and so mainly all they have in them is cigarette butts and sand. The other ones are worse. I'm saving them for last. I'm convinced that I'm going to find used condoms in them, or worse. I am supposed to note down the contents of each sample as precisely as possible.

Isaac and Katrina are watching me at my work, apparently fascinated, or maybe just wanting to procrastinate about whatever it is they're supposed to be doing.

"Here you go, babe—have another sample," says Katrina, offering me the butt from the cigarette she's just finished smoking.

"I don't want it! It'll mess up my data!" I carefully set a

Marlboro butt down next to one just like it. They both have the same color lipstick around the filter end, too—a possible correlation? I say, "Look at this guys: people who smoke Marlboros are more likely to wear really bright red lipstick."

"Hon, Sherlock Holmes has got nothing to worry about from you—those are obviously two butts smoked by the same person," says Katrina. "Look—you can see that the lipstick is lighter on the second butt, because some of it wore off on the first one."

"Or it could be that the lipstick was lighter on the first one, and then she reapplied it before she smoked the second one. Never thought of that, did ya?" says Isaac.

"You can't be sure it was a woman. Men wear lipstick sometimes," I say, thinking of the skirt-wearing boy.

Isaac has picked up one of the other plastic bags and is starting to screw around with it. He holds it up and says, "Exhibit A," trying to sound like a TV detective. He adds, "Ms. Lansdale, I think you'll agree with me that this conclusively proves that our murderer is a chain-smoking transvestite."

"Oh shit," says Katrina. This doesn't seem to be an appropriate response to Isaac's comment, so I look up from my notebook to see if there's something else she might be reacting to. That's when I see them. It's Battle.

And Kevin.

They're holding hands, and Battle is laughing.

"Give me that!" I snap at Isaac. He blinks, then quickly hands me the plastic bag. I snatch up all the other ones from the ground.

Then I run, across the courtyard and away. I don't stop, even though my breath is ragged and I'm crying, until I get close to the river.

I should have ripped open all the bags and dumped the garbage on their heads.

Katrina has been rationalizing for hours. I made her wait in my room with me until near the end of dinner before we went down, in case they were there. She says, "Sometimes people hold hands just because they're feeling friendly, you know. It doesn't necessarily mean the end of the world as we know it."

I pick up the straw that I got with my soda.

"Do you see this?" I ask.

"Yeah," she says.

"Do you recognize it?" I demand.

"It's a straw."

"Yes. It is also what you are grasping at for an explanation!"

I bite into my slice of pizza. My mouth fills with grease. "Makes me sick," I mutter, and spit out the bite of pizza into my napkin.

"Well hon, if it does, there's somebody you should be talking to about it, and it sure as shit isn't me," says Katrina.

"You mean the cook?" I ask. Katrina sighs.

"No, I do not mean the cook. I mean our friend Battle. I would just like to point out that all this trouble started at the point that you stopped talking to each other. There's also the fact that you haven't talked to me about what's behind all this, and there's a limit to the amount of help I can offer if you don't tell me what's really going on."

"Katrina—I can't. If you really want to know—and I want you to know, that's not the problem—you'll have to ask Battle, because it would be a betrayal of trust for me to tell you everything."

Just like it was a betrayal of trust for me to make up my own little soap opera about what happened when her brother ran away.

"Well, I'm not going to talk to her for you," she says.

"Did I ask you to?" I'm outraged. I rattle the ice in my glass, and then suck one of the cubes into my mouth. I bite down on it. It hurts my teeth. I keep chewing it until it dissolves and the water trickles down my throat.

Katrina throws up her hands. She says, "I give up. Look, I've got about a zillion hours of work to do before tomorrow morning. I'll be in my room if you need me." She gets up and leaves the table, abandoning her tray with the remains of her ranch-dressing-drowned salad.

I came to this program to study archaeology.

So goddammit, that is what I am going to do.

I unzip my backpack and take out one of my books.

After a minute or so, I'm suddenly flooded with panic. What if *they* decided to wait till near the end of dinner, too? So nobody would see *them?*

I have to get out of here.

I gulp the last of my Diet Coke and dump the tray in the garbage. Then I run back over for my backpack. I trip and hit my knee hard on a bench. It hurts a lot. I'll have a giant bruise.

Good.

Okay, I'm outside the dining hall and I haven't seen them yet. I should go back to my room using a different route than usual, in case they're on their way right now.

There's an elevator on the far left side of the hall. We never use it, but I found it once when I got disoriented on the way back from class.

I make a couple of wrong turns on the way to the elevator, and each time I turn a corner, my heart starts beating faster, until finally it feels like the big wooden metronome Ms. Edwards turns on sometimes during my viola lessons. "Allegro! Presto! Prestissimo!" And every time I see anyone coming down the hallway, I'm convinced for a split second that it's them.

I eventually resort to the strategy I used in elementary

school for deflecting insults. I get a book out of my back-pack and read it while I walk, only looking up when I absolutely have to. It would help if I could summon up some interest in Chapter 8 of *Discovering Our Past*, "Understanding the Past: Cultural Processual Reconstruction," but that's a bit too much to hope for.

Finally, I get to the elevator, and I stand in front of it for a few minutes, grateful to have gotten to it unscathed. I'm just about to press the button to call it when the doors slide apart.

She's got her back to me. That's because she's turned toward Kevin, who has his arms around her. Her head is tilted back.

They're kissing.

The only thing I can think of doing is to put the book so close to my face that maybe they won't recognize me when they get out of the elevator.

Kevin doesn't see me, but Battle does. She stares, her eyes huge.

I step into the elevator, press "Door Close," and sink down into the corner. I wrap my arms around my knees and my eyes begin to burn. I don't want to make any sounds. It hurts my throat not to sob, but I clench my jaw and hide my face between my knees

After a little while, I get up and push the button for my floor.

July 27, 10:30 a.m., Library

I thought that everything that could conceivably suck already did, but I'm wrong. Ms. Fraser wants to see me, so I must be failing archaeology. I wonder what my problem is. After all, if I can't get a relationship right, the least I should be able to do is learn about stratigraphy and systematics.

A blaze of freezing air conditioning hits me as I walk in, making goose bumps appear on my arms. I ask the guy at the desk where Ms. Fraser's office is.

"Up the stairs and to the left; it's the first carrel on the righthand side."

I hadn't even noticed there were stairs. But now that I know there are, I look up and see that there's a whole other level, a mezzanine. You could do a pretty decent *Romeo and Juliet* balcony scene from it. Not that I have anyone to play that scene with, now.

Ms. Fraser's reading the newspaper when I reach the cubicle. I clear my throat and say, "Hi."

"Nicola! I'm glad to see you," she says.

Glad? "You told me to come," I say, realizing belatedly that this sounds rude.

"Yes, I did. I told you to come to my spacious office." She extends her arms, and they touch the opposite walls of the cubicle. "But we don't have to stay here. I thought we could go for a walk."

I want to ask why, but she must have some kind of reason. Maybe she wants to show me some important thing about the soil here. "Okay."

We clump down the stairs. She's in front. There's graffiti on the walls on either side of the staircase. I read some of it in passing.

"*Zeppelin Rules*—hey, there's some data for future archaeologists," I say.

Ms. Fraser laughs. "Indeed. And if the music doesn't survive, they may well decide that there was a large cult devoted to an inefficient air travel vehicle."

I smile, but since she's in front, she can't see.

At the bottom of the stairs, Ms. Fraser pauses and looks up at me. She says, "Nicola, the reason I wanted you to come see me is that I'm worried about you. You haven't seemed yourself lately."

This is the last thing I expected.

I cross my arms over my chest and shrug.

"It's a hard class," I say, with that sinking feeling I always get when I know I've just said something stupid.

"Yes, it is. But I don't think that the class is what's hard for you right now," she says. "Let's get outside into the sunshine."

Our footsteps sound so loud on the old wooden stairs

that lead down and outside. It's like an echo chamber. *Thud, thud, thud.* It's dark in this stairwell, too. There's a little bit of light shining from underneath the big metal door at the bottom of the stairs. That door looks like an alarm will go off if you open it. Ms. Fraser pushes the bar forward, and it opens without any sound but the squeaking of hinges. It opens out into the courtyard.

Too many people like the courtyard. I saw Battle and Kevin on one of the benches there yesterday. I turned and ran.

"Can we walk more toward the river?" I ask.

"Certainly," says Ms. Fraser.

I'm glad she's not forcing me to talk. I don't know what to say. I don't know what she wants to hear. Maybe if I tell her why I'm upset she'll be sorry she ever asked.

It's sticky hot. For the first minute or two, I feel like I'm defrosting from the library air conditioning, and it's almost pleasant. Then my tank top starts sticking to me, and my jeans start to feel welded to my legs.

"I don't want to pry into your life, Nicola. I don't want you to feel that you have to share private things with me just because I'm your teacher. But you *can* talk, if you want to."

I sigh. I can feel tears starting to well up. It's like I've got a pressure gauge inside my head but I'm not in control of it, and when the pressure builds up too much the tears just gush right out. I haven't been looking where I'm going as we walk through the grass toward the river, and I slip on some goose shit and almost fall flat on my face. It's only by flailing my arms wildly that I manage not to fall over.

I say, and my voice comes out bitter and angry, "It's a story you've heard a zillion times. The cast of characters is different, that's all. There's two girls and a boy, but they're not in the roles you'd think they'd have."

Ms. Fraser says, "Ah." It's a very neutral "Ah"—it doesn't sound shocked or as though she suddenly understands the whole scenario. It's just "Ah."

I say, "But in a hundred years we'll all be dead so it doesn't matter."

Ms. Fraser says, "An archaeologist would say, in a hundred years we'll all be dead so it *does* matter."

"I don't even know if I want to *be* an archaeologist," I say. My voice reminds me of the way Isaac's sounded when he was saying he didn't even know where he was going to be living.

"You have a long time before you have to decide," says Ms. Fraser.

"You mean they don't kick you out of college if you don't know what you want to do right when you get there?" I ask.

Ms. Fraser laughs. "There are people who get through graduate school without knowing. I know someone who got his Ph.D. in philosophy and then became a mailman."

I say, "Listen, I really appreciate you being worried about me. But I'm going to be fine. Archaeology actually really helps. When I start thinking about people from thousands of years ago, what's happening to me now doesn't seem to matter all that much."

This is true, some of the time. Just not as often as I'd like.

Ms. Fraser gets a funny look on her face. "That's good—but don't go overboard with it. Don't use what you're studying as a way to get away from your feelings. It's not good for you."

I look at her, and wonder what she's thinking. "Okay," I say.

"Let's walk back," she says abruptly.

"Okay," I say again. "And thanks, again."

"I think of it as part of my job," says Ms. Fraser.

July 29, 2:40 p.m., Riverbank

"Well, *I* think you should come to San Francisco," says Isaac.

We've been talking, of course, about the phenomenon of Battle and Kevin. Katrina was going to come too, but at the last minute she said that she had too much work to do. This "masterwork for Carl," some giant program that she's writing, really seems to be taking over her existence. Apparently she hasn't even seen much of Battle and Kevin, because she's been taking all her meals up to her room. (And to judge from the trash that's been accumulating on her floor, most of said meals have been wrapped in plastic.)

It's colder today, amazingly enough, so I'm wearing a jacket over my T-shirt, and Isaac is wearing a baggy sweater over his.

"Why?" I ask, trying to put all of my irritation into that one word.

Isaac starts to say something, then coughs, then says in an overly manic way, "Because there are tons of dykes! I'm sure some of them would be just delighted to console you in your sorrow!"

"I think there's only one person who could console me now, Isaac, and it doesn't seem like she's at all inclined to do so. But I appreciate the thought." I sigh.

"I just have one question for you, Lancaster," Isaac says.

"What's that?" I ask.

"Since you first saw them holding hands that day, have you ever done anything other than run like hell when you've seen her coming—whether she's with Kevin or not? I'm not even talking about having a big conversation, I'm talking about something on the level of making *eye* contact with her. Have you?"

I glare at him. "You know I haven't. What's your point? Why should I put myself through more hell than I'm already going through?"

"Would you listen to yourself? Come on, Nic. This is the world's smallest violin," he says, rubbing his index finger over his thumb. "If you want to punch Kevin's lights out, I say go for it. If you want to give Battle a big old bitch-slap, I say go for that too. But turning around and running like you're Bambi's mom and they're the evil hunters is doing dick for you."

"Shut up. If you're so hot for direct action, why haven't you asked Katrina out yet?" I ask.

I know, of course, that the likelihood that Katrina would actually go out with him is close to nil, seeing as he's not a toadish-looking Computer Science teacher. But I don't want to tell him that.

He shrugs. "There are a lot of factors," he says, sounding uncomfortable.

I say, "Yeah, and one of them is that there's not a hell of a lot of time left, relatively speaking."

"Don't remind me," says Isaac. "I never thought I'd be dreading the end of PoliSci."

I realize belatedly that I've been self-centered during this entire conversation.

"Hey," I say softly. "You figured out where you and Rebecca are going to live yet?"

Isaac sighs, and rips up a patch of grass. Isaac Shawn, Destroyer of Lawns. "I think so."

"Where?" I pull one blade of grass carefully out of the ground, and put it between my lips.

"With Mom. She's going to stay in the old house, and that means we won't have to switch schools."

"Is your dad upset?" I ask. The blade of grass falls out of my mouth.

Isaac laughs, a bitter laugh. "Hardly. I think 'relieved' would be a more accurate representation of his feelings on the matter."

"Is he moving far away?" I ask.

"I don't think he knows what he's doing. He's so—" Isaac gropes for the right word, throwing a handful of grass up in the air. "He's so random. I mean for years, they didn't even *go* to temple, okay? And now all of a sudden he's like, 'Maybe I'll take some time off and go to Israel.' Well, bon fucking voyage, Dad—don't miss those settlements on the West Bank while you're there."

"I'm sorry," I say.

Isaac shrugs. "Not your fault he's an asshole."

We're quiet for a while, and I realize that we're sitting closer together than usual.

The silence gets louder and louder.

Something in the air changes, and I feel suddenly reckless, filled with a desperate desire for everything to become boy/girl simple. I lean in even closer to Isaac, kind of tilt my neck back and close my eyes, and sure enough, that's when he kisses me.

After a while, I break the kiss, and we blink at each other like cave-dwelling creatures who have stumbled mistakenly into the sunshine. Isaac clears his throat. "I've known that was going to happen for a long, long time," he says quietly.

"You *have?*" I squeak.

Isaac shrugs, of course. "I'm just not surprised," he says.

"Well, I am," I lie. Isn't this what I wanted? "I don't know what it means, what just happened." I move away from him.

Isaac cracks his knuckles, methodically, one by one. The silence extends.

"Well?"

Isaac cracks his wrists, then his neck.

"You're running out of joints," I point out.

He sighs. "It just makes sense, on a certain level," he says.

"*Why* does it make sense?" I tear my thumbnail off with my teeth. Nervous habits " Я " us.

Isaac shakes his head. "This is doing my male ego no good at all."

"Ha ha. So?" No blood this time. I'll have to try the other thumb.

"So neither of us can have who we really want," Isaac mumbles.

I stand up, furious. "You don't *know* you can't have Katrina, you haven't even *tried,* and besides, I don't want to *be,* or *have,* a consolation prize."

"I didn't say that!"

"Yes you did."

"Fine then, forget it. Walk away, pretend nothing happened." Isaac tries to crack his knuckles again, but they're all cracked out, so instead he takes off his glasses and polishes them with his shirt.

"That's not possible. It did, and I *still* don't know what it means."

"Jesus-crucified-Christ, Lancaster. If you didn't spend every goddamn second of your *life* trying to analyze the exact meaning of every single thing that ever *happened* to you, Battle might not have dumped you!"

A lump forms in my throat and my eyes sting. I rub my fists into them to banish the tears, but it does no good. "That wasn't fair," I almost whisper.

"I'm sorry, I'm sorry," Isaac mumbles. He stands up, and tentatively puts his arms around me.

We stand like that for a long time.

July 31, 4:47 p.m., My Room

<u>field notes</u>:
you said that words don't always work.
is that why you left me for that jerk?

no, doggerel doesn't help.
it's obvious that she'd rather be with kevin than with
me, and i don't really have any way of arguing with
that. i can't very well just say, "come back to me
because i have a bigger vocabulary and a better
sense of humor," because maybe she wants him
because he has muscular biceps and can play the
guitar.
and because he doesn't try to explain her life to her.

and because he's a boy.

katrina's always busy, and i haven't felt like i can
talk to isaac since that day at the river.

it's too complicated. i don't even know what i feel
any more.

so maybe i won't always be able to describe

165

precisely what i'm feeling. maybe i can't pin my feelings to the wall with neat little labels.

maybe i have to give up on having a typology of my emotions.

August 1, 6:00 a.m., Shower

I shut off first the hot, then the cold water. For a minute I stand dripping in the stall. Then I step out and grab my towel—and I'm face to face with Anne from my class, who's about to get into the shower next to mine.

"Hi," I say, wrapping my towel quickly around me. Anne looks startled, then says, "Oh, hi." We exchange embarrassed smiles, and then I notice that Anne looks more than startled. Her eyes are red, as though she's been crying.

"Hey, are you okay?" I ask. It's incredibly strange to be asking this question, while wearing only a towel, to another person who is also wearing only a towel. But Anne has been nice to me, and I want to be nice back.

"Oh, I'm fine," she says, and I can tell she's lying because her voice cracks a little on the word "fine."

"Are you sure? Because you seem pretty upset," I say. I would reach out a hand to put on her shoulder, but then my towel would fall.

166

"I'll be fine—I just need to take a shower!" she says, dismissing me.

"Okay—well, I guess I'll see you on the bus," I say.

This is the day we visit an in-progress dig. I'm pleased—it will get me away from everyone.

Obviously Anne's not fine, I think as I get dressed. I yank my brush through my hair and tie it back. Maybe I'll ask her about it on the way there.

After I get coffee and a bagel, I end up being one of the first people to arrive at the place where the bus is waiting. Unfortunately, the people who have gotten there before me are Ben and Alex. I attempt to ignore them, wishing I'd brought a book.

"Oooh, Little Miss Bleeding Heart Lesbian's by herself today," says Ben. "Did China Girl turn you down?"

"What the hell are you talking about?" I demand.

Ben grins. He says, "You know what I'm talking about. I know about you—I've seen you around with that other girl, the skinhead. Well, she ditched you, so now you wanna put some Chinese food on your menu."

"Moo goo *gay* pan," Alex chimes in.

Elementary school. I'm totally back in elementary school. I never talked back, I just let them insult me until they got bored and left. But they're not going to leave, they're waiting to go to the same place I am. And of course, my face is doing its usual impersonation of an overripe tomato.

Dammit. I have to say something.

I say, "Boy, you guys are going to make *super* archaeologists. You'll write really sensitive analyses of oppressed cultures."

God, that was a stupid thing to say.

"Oh, we're all about sensitivity. We think that people like you should be given every opportunity to return to normal—like your girlfriend did," says Ben.

"Shut the fuck up," I say, a lump beginning to form in the back of my throat. I will be damned if I let myself cry in front of them. I go on, "And hey, why do I always see *you* guys together all the time?"

Somewhere underneath my anger and fear, I'm amused to see Alex take a step away from Ben.

"Doughnut?" a voice asks from behind me. It's Ms. Fraser, and she's holding two big boxes from the campus bakery.

"No thanks," I say, absolutely relieved.

"I figured that since I was making you all get up so early, it was the least I could do. Sure you don't want one?" she asks.

"I have a bagel, thanks."

"Boys?" she asks, turning to Alex and Ben. They each take a giant cream puff, which strikes me as entirely appropriate. In a minute, their mouths are both smeared with the viscous yellow-white doughnut filling.

More people begin to arrive before too much longer, and I drift farther and farther out of range of the doughnut-eating homophobes. Eventually, Anne turns up. If I didn't already know that she was upset earlier, it would be hard to tell now. "Hey, how are you doing?" I ask.

Anne sighs. She appears to be going through some kind of struggle, presumably about whether or not she can share her problem with me.

"Promise not to tell anyone," she says.

I nod. Who would I tell?

"My boyfriend—he broke up with me, yesterday. He called me and said he met someone else at the pool where he works. And he wanted to still be friends! I hung up on him."

"And it just came right out of the blue like that?" I ask.

She nods. "I mean, there was one time when I called and his mom said he was working, but I didn't think anything of it—he's always taken as many hours as they'll give him at the pool. He really likes lifeguarding."

"Lots of bikinis," I say cynically.

"He didn't used to be that way!" she cries. Then she says more softly, "I think—I think maybe if I hadn't come here, we'd still be together."

"Okay—everybody on! Let's get this show on the road!" says Ms. Fraser. Anne and I get in line with everyone else, and make our way onto the bus. We find seats near the back. I note with relief that Alex and Ben are sitting up near the front—perhaps the better to harass the driver.

"You can't second-guess yourself like that," I say once we're sitting down. "I mean, he'd still have been doing the lifeguard job whether you were here or at home. He would probably still have met the other girl, regardless."

"I just don't think it would have happened if I'd been at home. He didn't want me to go, you know. He said it was a waste of summer to go to some nerd tank," she says. She takes an apple out of the brown paper sack she's been carrying and bites into it.

"It sounds like he was intimidated by your intelligence. Hey, I know you don't think so now, but you're probably better off. I bet he was holding you back." It's amazing how easy it is for me to fling these platitudes around.

"But I still love him!" she says.

"Yeah. I know how you feel. I got dumped this summer, too," I say, realizing belatedly that this may have been a really stupid thing to bring up.

"You did? I didn't even know you were dating anybody. Was it somebody here, or back home?" she asks, suddenly interested, taking another bite of her apple.

I forgot that it's always compelling for somebody who's upset to focus on someone else's problems for a while. I think I forgot because I was being compelled by Anne's problem to stop focusing on mine.

Damn. Truth or lie? Oh, the hell with it.

"Here," I say.

"Do I know him?" she asks.

I shake my head. "I don't think so. And just so you know, you may not want to associate with me anymore—it wasn't a him. It was a her."

Anne looks at me for a minute. "I'm straight," she says nervously. "I mean, just in case you were thinking—I mean, it doesn't bother me or anything, but you know, you should just be aware that I'm straight."

"I know," I say. "I'm glad it doesn't bother you."

If I were really mean, I would give her a hug right now. But then she'd have a heart attack.

"She ditched me for a guy," I say. "That was the worst thing about it."

"I'm sorry," Anne says.

We sit in silence for a while. The motion of the bus also reminds me of elementary school. Fortunately, the bus doesn't have the elementary school bus smell, which always seemed to consist in approximately equal parts of sack lunches and vomit. This is actually a pretty deluxe bus. The seats are covered in cloth instead of vinyl, and they don't have bits picked off of them the way the seats always did on the buses at home. And there doesn't seem to be nearly as much gum stuck under the seats.

"When you met her," asks Anne, evidently consumed by curiosity, "how did you, like, know?"

For a moment, I have no idea what she's talking about. Then I say, "Oh, you mean how did I know she was queer? I just flashed the universal hand signal."

"Oh," says Anne. Then I take pity on her.

"I'm kidding. There isn't really a hand signal. I don't know how I knew—how does anybody ever know?" What, no analysis? No documentation, no diagrams? Ms. Lancaster, are you quite well?

The bus goes over a large bump in the road. I hope Alex and Ben are feeling queasy now after those doughnuts. I sip my coffee, which is lukewarm but still good.

"Love just sucks," says Anne.

"Yeah," I say. "Let's put our careers first like the modern women we are."

"Right on," says Anne. After a minute, though, she shakes her head and says, "No, I can't do it. I want both. I need a challenging career *and* a fulfilling love life." She sounds like somebody on a TV talk show, and I can't quite tell whether or not she's doing it on purpose.

"Well you know," I say thoughtfully, "there's still some time left in the program. It would be great if you hooked up with somebody here and could write him a letter agreeing that yeah, you should just be friends because you're really infatuated with Pierre, or whoever."

Anne begins to giggle. "That would be cool," she says. "Except that I never see any guys except the ones in class— bleah."

Alex and Ben are merely the worst in a class of male zeroes.

"Bleah indeed. Couldn't you catch someone's eye in the cafeteria?" I ask.

"Oh yeah—while you're eating is always *such* a good time to meet guys," Anne says sarcastically.

"Well, do you do anything else?"

Anne thinks for a minute. "I go to the gym and do the Stairmaster in the morning."

"There you go! There's got to be somebody there for you. All that sweat and energy—you can't lose!" I say this as though I actually darken the door of any gym voluntarily.

Anne says, "Hmmm, there are a couple of hotties there. I never really let myself notice them before, but now . . . all right. I will not be wounded!" She's sounding like a talk show person again, but this time I'm pretty sure she's putting it on.

"You will survive," I say, trying to use the same overly emotional kind of voice. We laugh.

At the front of the bus, Ms. Fraser stands up. "I need your attention!" she yells. The bus ride seems to be making us all a lot noisier than usual. Slowly, we quiet down.

"I want to tell you some things about the site we're going to see. This is an excavation of an Iroquois longhouse, and it's an *area* excavation. Somebody tell me, is that a common kind of excavation?"

"No!" various people yell.

"Why not?" she asks.

" 'Cause it's too expensive!"

"That's right. These folks have gotten a large grant, and that's what's allowing them to do this project. In fact, if any of you are wondering how you're going to spend *next* summer, I happen to know that they're looking for people to help out," Ms. Fraser says.

Next summer? I can barely think about next *week*.

Another of the guys, whose name I can never remember, raises his hand. "Would they pay us?" he asks.

"Not much, if anything. But it would look very good on a college application," says Ms. Fraser. Those are the magic words.

Ms. Fraser goes on. "You're going to meet the director of the dig. His name is Peter Francis—Dr. Francis—and I'm not sure if he's going to show you around himself or if he'll have one of his assistants do it, but either way, remember that they're doing me, and you, a big favor by letting us observe today, and please act accordingly."

"So don't step on any artifacts!" somebody yells. A few people laugh.

174

"We'll be having lunch on site with the rest of the team—I'm hoping that will give you an opportunity to talk to some of the students—and we'll be coming back in enough time for you to get dinner in the dining hall. I can't encourage you enough to ask any questions you have; the team will be happy to answer them. Do you have any questions now?"

Silence. "All right, I'll assume you're holding all your brilliant queries until we get there—which should be in another ten or fifteen minutes. At ease," she says, and sits back down in her seat.

Anne is still adjusting to the concept that she's actually free to look around. "John and I were together for so long—it was like, over a year—I don't know if I even remember how to flirt!" She giggles, then looks suddenly penitent. "I don't know about this, Nicola—I mean, maybe this chick is just a summer fling for John. What if I come back with a new boyfriend and then I find out he wants me back? What'll I do then?"

This conversation is fascinating. I never suspected that this was the person lurking underneath Anne's cool and collected exterior. I say, "I think it would serve him right if you did. He was toying with your affections. Besides, you can always break up with your new guy to go back to John if you really want to."

"That's true," Anne muses. "But now I'm going to have to wear only *nice* stuff to the gym—like color-coordinated workout gear! I don't know if I can handle it."

"I'm sure you'll be fine," I say.

For a moment, I entertain the concept of following my own advice. But I don't even know if I'd be looking for a girl or a boy, let alone how to attract the object of my hypothetical affection once I found it. Besides, the idea of trying to pick up some random person just so I can stop feeling shitty about Battle strikes me as morally questionable, even if I could somehow manage to do it.

Well, what about Isaac?

I think about the kiss, try to remember exactly what it felt like—and I can't.

I can remember standing in his arms, afterwards, crying, but the kiss itself is like something I saw in a movie. Whereas everything that happened with Battle has been seared into my brain with a branding iron. Does that mean I'm definitely a lesbian, not bisexual, or just that I love Battle and I only like Isaac?

Maybe you don't get to know, Nic. Maybe you need to stop trying to pick it all apart.

The bus begins to shudder to a stop, and I look out of the window.

It's not a parking lot per se, it's more sort of a wider-than-normal dirt road. It must be miserable when it rains.

There are four or five cars all clustered together at one end of it, as though they're whispering to each other.

I look beyond the parking area and all I see is a large grassy open field. It looks like one of the places you drive by all the time on country roads, that always end up having a sign somewhere that says "5,000 Acres for Sale or Lease," or "Jesus Died for Your Sins." Or "Clean Fill Dirt Wanted."

Anne and I stand up and stretch. "Doesn't look like much, does it?" I ask.

"I think the main part where people are working is over that way," Anne says, pointing in the opposite direction from where I'd been looking. There's still a fair amount of grassy field, but beyond it I can just see a pile of dirt, and a large area that's been roped off into a grid, the way I've seen in the illustrations of our archaeology books. People are moving around in various sections of the grid. It has sort of an anthill quality, although I suspect that effect is enhanced by the pile of dirt.

I find it very hard to focus on the tour Dr. Francis is giving us. He reminds me of Large Pink Bald Man from the convocation at the beginning of summer, which feels like a million years ago. I wish he'd just shut up and let Ms. Fraser talk. He's telling us all this useless garbage about how they wrote the grant and the other projects they were competing against for the money. He says, "This is the first time in over a decade that an area excavation of this magnitude has been funded to this level. It reflects a true understanding of the importance of our site by the foundation."

Why don't you tell us about what people are *doing,* instead of about how impressive it is that you got the money to do it? I look over at Anne to see if she's bored too, but whether she is or not, she's totally absorbed in taking notes in her little leather notebook.

Because this talk is so abysmally boring, I start to wonder if Anne's note-taking is anything like mine. I try to catch a glimpse of the page she's working on, and I can only see a few words: "green Adidas—yes." She's planning her gym wardrobe!

I bet I can learn more by looking around than by watching Large Pink Dr. Francis while he pontificates. He's been talking an amazingly long time without saying anything. So I shift my focus over to one of the grid squares where people are working—and freeze. That's *Battle* over there!

I look again, and realize that no, it isn't, it couldn't be— Battle doesn't have long hair any more. But this woman, whoever she is, has hair that looks just like Battle's did at the beginning of the summer. She has her back to me, so I look at her for a few more minutes. Then she turns around, as though she's seen me looking.

She's a guy. A long-haired, blue-eyed, cute guy, who's sifting dirt through a screen to find the smallest artifacts. He gives me a big smile and waves. Blushing, I wave back, imagining telling him, "I'm sorry for staring, but you look just like my ex-girlfriend from the back."

Suddenly, what Dr. Francis is saying penetrates my consciousness. "I think we'll be having an early lunch today so you all will be sure to have some time to interact with the team. Team, please show our visitors where they can find lunch."

There's scattered cheering among the people working, which gives rise to scattered cheers among our group. The guy who isn't Battle puts down his screen and starts walking over to me. When he reaches where Anne and I are standing, he extends his hand and says, "Hey, I'm Doug, and you are?"

"Nicola," I say. Not Nic. "And this is my friend Anne."

Anne looks up from her notebook and smiles hugely. She must also think Doug is cute.

"Well hello, Nicola and Anne—congratulations on surviving that speech. Dr. Francis is a good guy, but you get him in front of a group of people and he just goes into fund-raising mode. What you heard was just about exactly what he says to people who are visiting because they want to donate money to the project. I think he forgot you guys were coming today. Where are you from, again?"

"The Siegel Institute," says Anne. Doug looks confused for a minute, then says, "Oh yeah! I always forget that they host that at Prucher in the summer. Hey, you know, I went there for undergrad. I love Prucher Hall. Do they still have all those great trees in the courtyard?"

"Yeah!" I say, warming to Doug. "They're totally excellent for climbing."

Doug nods enthusiastically. "Oh man, I *loved* climbing those trees! The best thing was to climb one late at night and smoke a bowl—oops, should I be saying that to you guys?"

Anne and I laugh. "I guess your RAs weren't really strict," I say.

"Man, I *was* an RA," says Doug. "But it was a while back. Things are probably different now. It's so cool that's where you guys are from! Well, follow me over this way and I'll show you our fine dining selections."

Doug walks in front of us, and he looks like Battle again. It's uncanny.

"I think he's flirting with you," Anne whispers. "Are you mad?"

I look at her, confused. "I don't know if he is or not," I whisper back, "but why would I be mad?"

"Because he's a guy!" Anne whispers more loudly.

"Oh! No, that wouldn't make me mad," I say.

Anne shakes her head. Obviously, I keep failing to act the way she expects.

Doug is leading us across the parking area toward a small white vehicle that looks sort of like an ice cream truck.

180

"O'Riley's Food Service" is painted on one side in bright blue letters. "These guys come every day that we're here. Their stuff's not bad, but a lot of us bring our own lunches and keep them in the coolers over there." He nods toward a spot over in the tall grass where there are several wooden picnic tables in addition to four large orange coolers.

"Were those here when you guys started?" I ask, pointing at the tables.

"No, they weren't—one of the donors gave them. Dr. Francis was really angry, because we're just going to have to take them down once we finish, and they don't do us any good, and they cost a lot more than you'd expect. It's nice to have somewhere to sit for lunch, but in the grand scheme of things it's fairly gratuitous."

Anne and I get in line for O'Riley's Food Service while Doug gets his lunch out of one of the coolers. As we approach the front of the line, I see that it's apparently run by the Mexican branch of the O'Rileys.

By the time we have our food, all the tables are filled. Doug says, "If you don't mind sitting on the ground, there's a nice shady spot over a little closer to the dig. Just don't leave any garbage!"

The three of us walk over to Doug's spot, which is underneath a giant oak tree. I sprawl out on my stomach, as does Doug. Anne sits cross-legged against the trunk of the tree.

"How long have you been doing archaeology?" I ask

Doug, taking a bite of my tostada. It's quite good, particularly in comparison to what the dining hall likes to think of as Mexican food.

Doug rests his chin on his right hand and looks up as though the answer to my question is somewhere in the clouds overhead. "Uh . . . well, let's see. Did my first dig back in undergrad, so that would've been . . . Jesus, I guess it's ten years now."

"You don't look that old," Anne says, and then blushes.

Doug laughs. "Thanks!" he says. He takes a banana, a Tupperware bowl, and a fork out of his lunch sack.

"Did you know for a long time that this is what you wanted to do?" I ask.

Doug shakes his head. "I got my undergrad in anthro, but I didn't know what I was going to do with it. The first dig I went on, I got onto because I was dating somebody who was on it."

"That's so random!" I say. I don't know if these are the kinds of questions Ms. Fraser wanted us to ask, but I'm very interested in Doug's answers.

"Yeah, I know. Funny, isn't it? If I'd known when I started how much lab work there is in proportion to stuff like this, I don't know if I would have gotten into it. I might have been a forest ranger instead."

I'm slightly appalled. "But aren't you interested in the analysis?" I ask.

"Oh, definitely! But that doesn't mean it's fun to sit in the lab doing testing on soil samples, or spectrographic analysis on a pottery fragment. You have to be willing to put up with the scut work if you want to get into this."

"Ms. Fraser was telling us that it's kind of hard to get jobs," Anne says.

Doug peels his banana. "It is. But it's not that bad. What happens is that you get to know people, and then when they're going to write up grants for projects, they let you know, and you get included in their grant proposal."

"It seems like it's a lot more about money than I thought it would be," I say.

"Everything is, Nicola," says Doug, taking a large bite out of his banana.

August 6, 11:42 p.m., My Room

field notes:
positive things since the end of me and battle:
1. talking with anne on bus
2. finding out about archaeology from doug (who asked for my e-mail address)
3. a couple of evenings with katrina before she got so obsessive about her giant programming project
4. walking by the river with isaac, except for the weird kiss thing

. . . but none of these really signify. i'm walking around with a giant hole in the middle of my chest. i'm just trying to ignore it and hope that everyone else does too.

nicola lancaster's brain is:

the skin underneath a scab someone's just ripped off. pink and raw and painful and likely to get infected.

problem w/ this analogy:

skin underneath a scab isn't capable of being stupid.

i just want to hide, and run away, and be anywhere in the entire world but wherever she is. except that part of me still wants to be with her more than to be anywhere else.

talking to ms. fraser was a good thing, i guess, but it didn't change anything. maybe i'll get a better grade because she feels sorry for me, but that's it. didn't bring battle back. didn't strangle kevin with one of his guitar strings.

dominant feeling: anger, at self, this was supposed to be a summer class in archaeology, not some idiotic soap opera mess. [except that no soap operas would have a love affair between girls as a storyline, unless one of us died tragically in a car crash, and then *the other one was comforted in her grief by some charming young man.]*

damn it.

this isn't helping.

I close my notebook. Perhaps, in honor of Doug, I should climb the big tree in the courtyard, though I have no bowl to smoke.

It's chilly tonight, though. It doesn't feel like summer at all. I'll need my sweater.

I have my hand on the sweater before I remember what's underneath it.

I remember I thought it felt like a rope. But is it enough rope to hang myself? God, Nic, stop being so melodramatic. I lift out Battle's braid along with my sweater. I didn't use much of it to make the Empress. She's under the sweater, too.

I study archaeology. They're artifacts.

I open my notebook again, and turn to a blank page. Since Battle left me, I've been playing my viola a lot, but I haven't drawn at all, except for class. I put the mass of hair and the Empress on my bed, and begin to sketch them.

Really, all the braid is, is pattern. The subtle gradations of color, the way it catches the light, the curves created by the braiding. If I squint my eyes just right, I can forget it was ever attached to someone I love.

Except for that very faint scent of lavender.

Suddenly there's a very loud banging on my door. "Open up, in the name of the law!" It's Katrina.

"Hold on," I say, picking up the braid and the Empress and tossing them back into the drawer. "Okay, come in, what's up?"

"I'll tell you what's up, what's up is that we are going to go commit an act of sabotage right now, and 'we' *does* in fact mean you *and* me *and* Battle, and I don't care how angsty you feel, I am sick of dealing with your bullshit, you are going to go and get her right now, or else I will stand here and sing 'Climb Every Mountain' over and over and over again, until you go *insane!*"

"I thought you still had that massive programming project," I say.

"Well! You thought wrong, little missy! I've left all that behind me! Carl Sutter the Evil Toad can just kiss my big fat hairy white *butt!*"

Her eyes are red-rimmed with dark circles under them, her hair is standing on end. Her "If I Had Known Grandchildren Were So Much Fun, I Would Have Had Them First" T-shirt looks like she's been wearing it for days.

"How long have you been awake, Katrina?"

She looks at her giant digital watch. "Thirty-seven hours, twenty-three minutes, and fourteen! fifteen! sixteen! seconds! Now it's seventeen! Why do you ask? Why aren't you going to get Battle? Climb . . . . eeeee-vr'y moun-tain! Ford . . . . eeee-vr'y streeeeeem!"

I hear doors opening all up and down the hall. "Shut up!" someone yells.

"Would it be completely useless for me to ask you to calm down?" I ask.

"Yes! It would! That was perceptive! You! Are! So! Perceptive! That it's! Amazing!" She sounds like somebody in a Lynda Barry cartoon.

"Katrina, are you on drugs?"

"No! I just get high on life! And America! Are you going to go get Battle or not? FO-LLOW EEEEV'RY RAIN-BOW!!"

Katrina can't sing. At all.

"Shut up, just for a second! What's really going on?"

"Nothing's going *on!* I'm going *off!* Pow! Like a bomb!"

"Is this some bizarre strategy to get me to talk to Battle?"

"Oh, you, you, you, why does everything always have to be about *you?* Daaarr-ling, we don't have much time! Carpe carpem! *Seize* the carp!"

"So why don't you come with me to get Battle?"

"Because, silly—somebody has to get the supplies together! I'm off! Be at my room in ten minutes, with Battle, or I'll come back here and start in on the John Denver!"

She flounces out of the room.

Now what?

Even if I was going to go along with this psychotic

episode Katrina seems to be having, it's past midnight. Battle's probably asleep.

Guess you'll just have to wake her up, then! Katrina's voice says in my head.

Well—what the hell. What do I have to lose?

It's not like she can *leave* me.

Deus ex Katrina.

Just act natural, I think as I knock on the door, with my tell-tale heart beating loudly enough to wake Poe from the dead.

The door opens. She's holding the book I gave her.

"Hi . . . did I wake you?"

She shakes her head. Her hair's longer, almost to crew-cut length. She looks tired.

"Katrina wants us for something. She wouldn't explain what. She's been up for almost two days straight, and she's pretty scary right now," I sound astonishingly normal.

"All right." So does she. "Let me put some pants on." She stands in the doorway for a minute, obviously debating whether she should invite me in.

"I'll wait."

I look at the carpet. It's dull gray with tiny black diamonds. Probably they picked it because they thought it wouldn't show the dirt. I wonder how many diamonds there are per square foot.

"Okay, let's go." She's wearing the jodhpurs that she wore the night we went to the woods.

Don't look at *her*, doofus. Look at all those fascinating tiny black diamonds on the carpet.

The distance between Battle's room and Katrina's has never seemed so far.

I'm so relieved when we get to her door that I don't hear it immediately.

"All right, we're here, what do you want us to do?" I call out.

"I don't think she wants us to do anything. Listen," says Battle.

Battle and I used to try to get Katrina to come to breakfast with us, and it was always an ordeal, because Katrina sleeps more deeply and snores louder than anyone I've ever met. And it's that irregular, snorting sound that I hear now, through her door.

"Oh, god. She must have crashed." I lean against the doorway, my legs suddenly rubbery.

"Sounds like she needed to."

"Yeah, she definitely did."

Now what?

We stand outside Katrina's room for five minutes, listening to her snore.

"So," I say, finally. "Hi."

My voice sounds weird and hollow.

"Hi," says Battle.

Her voice sounds just like mine, except shakier.

It would take more than a knife to cut this tension. It would require at least a chainsaw. The thought of brandishing a chainsaw strikes me funny, and I want to tell Battle, and I look up at her for an instant before I remember that I can't tell her, because that would be acknowledging that the tension exists. It's in that instant that I see the tears running down her cheeks.

"Come on. Let's not talk in the hallway," I say abruptly.

Without waiting to see if she follows me, I start walking back to my room. And I hear her footsteps behind me, and her breathing.

I unlock my door and sit down on the floor, my back against the bed. I start pulling out a loose thread from the bedspread.

She sits on the floor, too, on the other side of the room. She runs her hands through her hair distractedly. I can feel it as though it were my hands in the soft blonde fuzz.

I have no idea what I'm going to say to her. The tears are starting to come for me, too, and the lump in my throat. Damn it. I don't care any more.

"I love you," I say. It sounds like I'm saying, "Fuck you," because my voice is so angry.

She just looks at me.

I wrap the loose thread from the bedspread around the

index finger of my left hand, tightly enough to cut off the circulation. I watch my fingertip slowly turn from red to purple.

"I love you, too." She enunciates this very carefully, like a mother speaking to the child who's just broken her favorite vase.

"Oh sure—'as a friend,' right?" I accuse her with the biggest cliché of teenage romance.

"Yes—but that's not all, and you know it." Now she sounds angry, too.

"Do I? How about Kevin? What does he know?" I let go of the thread, and the blood throbs back into my finger.

"Kevin is not relevant," Battle says coldly.

"Oh, really? Well, he seemed pretty goddamned relevant to you in the elevator! Not to mention all those times you went strolling all over campus hand in hand."

She expels her breath quickly—it's too explosive to be called a sigh.

"Well?" I demand.

Battle says, sounding incredibly irritated, "Look, I can't give you a perfect explanation."

"Did I say I wanted one?"

She looks straight at me and says simply, "You always do."

All the anger rushes out of me and is immediately replaced by shame.

"Whatever you want to say or do is fine." I try to keep my voice neutral, but it comes out small and pathetic-sounding. My eyes hurt in a way that's half wanting to cry and half simple fatigue. This makes me realize just how tired I am, how little sleep I've gotten since Battle left me, how drained I already was when Katrina showed up at my door. What I really want right now is for us to hurry up and finish reconciling.

There's a long silence. I shiver. My fatigue has made me cold; I can see the goose bumps on my legs. But I don't feel like pulling the blanket off the bed. That would be too comforting, and that's not what I want right now.

"What if I don't have a good reason for what happened with Kevin?" Battle's voice is low.

"What do you mean? What would a good reason have been?"

I don't know what she's getting at. I'm trying not to sound angry, but I don't think it's working.

Battle sits silent again for a minute and then says all in a rush, "A good reason would have been that I didn't care about you any more."

"But you said you didn't have a good reason."

She nods.

This is ridiculous. We're not communicating, we're having a contest to see who can be more indirect. Words really *don't* work, do they? Without meaning to, I start to laugh, and once I start, I can't stop. This must be hysteria.

"Why are you laughing?"

I wheeze a few times and manage eventually to get enough breath to say, "Us. We're acting like teenagers, you know." My voice is shaky. At a certain point, it really is hard to tell the difference between laughing and crying.

"We *are* teenagers," Battle reminds me.

"I know. But this is so dumb."

"Dumb—uh oh, that's dangerous. Think they'll kick us out?" Battle's voice is . . . edgy? Brittle? I can't think of the right word.

"Kick us out? Isn't it a little late for that?" I don't know where she's going with this.

"For being dumb. We're at a gifted program, get it?" She tries to laugh, for about three seconds. Then she just looks at me. Battle has more eyes than other people. It's like everyone else's eyes are sixty watts and hers are a million. I look away.

"You don't hold anything back, do you?" she asks in a flat voice.

"Should I?"

She sighs. It's as though she's thoroughly exasperated that telepathy doesn't work. That I can't read whatever the neon sign she thinks she has flashing on her forehead is saying. Is this a Southern thing, to expect people to understand you without you actually having to *say* anything?

I wait.

"It just doesn't seem to be hard for you." She's talking to the floor, not to me. But then again, that's where I'm looking.

"What doesn't?"

"Intimacy." She does look up when she says that.

"Should it be?"

"It is for most of us."

"Doesn't seem like it was that hard for you with *Kevin.*"

She laughs a short laugh that's almost a bark. "I think I said a total of twenty words to Kevin during our involvement, and ten of them were 'Really?' He doesn't know I have a brother, he doesn't know why I shaved my head, he doesn't even know I have *dogs.*"

"What does he know?"

Battle shrugs, reminding me of Isaac. "That I'll listen to him blather about composition for hours on end. Oh, and that I'm a 'babe,' apparently."

I smile, just a little. "Well, you are."

"Nic—you knew more about me in an hour than he learned in weeks. Do you have any idea how scary that is?"

I don't know what to say, so I just look at her, and she says all in a rush, "It felt sometimes like you wanted to *vivisect* me, like you wouldn't be happy until you had everything about me classified, labeled, and put into jars with formaldehyde."

"You don't have to believe this, but I'm trying not to do that anymore," I say.

"I don't know what I believe."

"Neither do I."

We look at each other.

Maybe I shouldn't try to label everything I feel, but right now, it's definitely love.

"We'd better get some sleep." Why did I say that?

She nods. Then she gets up, crosses the room, and awkwardly reaches out to give me a hug.

I don't want to let go, but at the same time, I have to. I don't have room left for any more emotions tonight. So after a moment, I step away, and say "Sleep well."

"Sleep well," she echoes from the doorway, and closes the door behind her.

In the morning, I call Isaac's room. Phones are easier.

"Battle and I talked last night."

"Good. Took you long enough."

"We're not back together or anything, but I don't think she's with Kevin anymore, either."

"That's good too."

"Now all you have to do is ask Katrina out!"

"I don't *have* to do anything, Lancaster. Except finish this paper."

"Sorry—I didn't mean it that way. Isaac?"

"I'm listening."

"I'm sorry I got so weird about what happened at the river."

"It's all right."

"Are you sure?"

"Yeah."

"Thanks—thanks for being my friend, Isaac."

"Don't go getting all sentimental on me, Lancaster. I've gotta fight the Six-Day War in ten pages by four P.M."

I have to laugh. "Huh. How many days was *our* war, I wonder?"

"It doesn't matter now. Does it?"

August 9, 4:12 p.m., My Room

field notes:

katrina claims not to remember what she wanted the three of us to do so desperately.

she doesn't even clearly remember coming to my room. what she does remember is that about halfway through debugging her massive programming project, her crush on carl "just curled up and died like a dog," at which point the whole debugging process became far less interesting, seeing as it was no longer a labor of love, so to maintain her alertness, she slammed coke and chain-smoked until she was out of cigarettes. but at some point she just lost it, and she guesses that's when she came to my room.

she felt so gross when she finally woke up that she is quitting smoking.

other changes in the group dynamic:

—haven't seen kevin for days (yay!)

—isaac is flirting with katrina much more blatantly now, and she is actually flirting back

—battle and i are . . . mostly just acting like really close friends, which we are, regardless of whatever else we might be.

but there are moments. one of us touches the other without thinking about it, and then pulls her hand back. one of us makes a comment with a double entendre, and we both blush. we haven't talked at all about what we want to be to each other. i don't think either of us knows. and besides (one more time): words don't always work.

Battle is compiling her notes for a World History paper—only Battle could be so organized that she can get everything in order while she's sitting in a tree—and I'm trying to write the analysis of the four artifacts Ms. Fraser has borrowed from the dig for us to study. Right now, I'm just staring at the pictures I drew of them in my notebook. I've gotten so much more practice drawing this summer than I thought I would.

I yawn, stretch, and look down. There was a Frisbee game going on earlier, but the players have now disappeared. It was fun to follow the game from above, watching the red disc sail through the air from one end of the courtyard to the other.

Two figures come out of the double doors that lead into the dining hall.

"Free at last, free at last, great God almighty, I'm free at last!" the first figure yells, throwing her hands up into the air. The first figure is Katrina. The second figure, I note with delight, is Isaac.

"Battle, check this out!" I whisper up to her. She's sitting on a slightly higher branch than I am this time. I point at Isaac and Katrina, and Battle grins hugely.

"So that's your last big assignment?" asks Isaac. They sit down on one of the benches, fortunately still within earshot. If they looked up, they would see us. But they don't.

Katrina says, "Yup, that's right, only tiny little stupid projects for Mr. Toad till the end of the term!" She's talking faster and louder than usual.

"She's nervous," Battle whispers down to me.

"I know," I whisper back.

"Hey, you know what else?" Katrina says, in that same manic voice. "It's been a week. I've been clean for a week. No nicotine has entered my bloodstream, no tar has defiled my lungs. They say you keep smelling like smoke for a while after you quit. Do you think I still smell like smoke?"

She leans her head very close to Isaac's, and he sniffs the top of her head solemnly. "I can't quite tell," he says seriously. Katrina looks up at him. She says, "Well, then tell me if I taste like smoke." And then she puts her arms around him and kisses him.

Battle and I immediately start making the kinds of noises that seventh-grade boys make in movies when the heroine takes off her shirt.

"Wheeeeoooooo!"

"Ow, ow, ow!"

They stop kissing and look up, aghast.

"Wish I had a camera with me, that was such a Kodak moment!" I yell down.

Isaac frowns at Katrina. "Were you in with them on this?" he demands furiously. Katrina shakes her head vigorously. "I had no idea they were up there—you bitches! No idea at all."

Isaac stands up, craning his neck back to look at us. He shakes his finger and says, "You are so dead. You don't even *know* how dead you are. Soon as you come down out of that tree, you are not even going to remember what it was like having all your limbs attached in the proper places." He almost cracks up as he says this last sentence, but he tries to maintain a tough-guy voice.

"Aw, come on, Isaac, I'm sure you can think of something *better to do* than wait for us to come down!" I'm so pleased I can hardly contain myself. If I could dance from up here, I would.

Isaac pretends to consider this for a minute. "Do I? Do I have anything better to do, Katrina?"

And Katrina grabs hold of his arm and begins dragging him out of our view.

August 16, 7 p.m., Cafeteria

"This is the lamest thing I've ever seen," Isaac says at dinner on Saturday, brandishing a flyer that was put under all of our doors earlier in the week. The hot pink flyer advertises, in cutesy-looking handwriting, an end-of-term dance, to take place tonight. "They figure we don't get enough of this shit at our regular schools, or what?"

"Oh, come on, honey, don't you want to dance with me to all the slow songs?" Katrina asks in a sickly-sweet voice, batting her eyelashes.

Isaac says, "Nic and Battle, you guys should take the floor. Do a total gropefest and see if they try to stop you. If they do, you can slap an anti-discrimination suit on them and make a lot of money."

"Not my idea of fun on a Saturday night," says Battle. I nod. I could kick Isaac. He ought to know that things are still way up in the air with the two of us. I also suspect that San Francisco Boy has no idea that there are people here who would act like Alex and Ben did. I haven't told anyone about that.

"Oh, come on you guys, it's an excuse to dress up!" says Katrina.

"Like you need one," says Isaac.

Of course, Katrina manages to convince us all that we should go, and that we can always leave if it's too awful. She wants to do makeup for everyone, even Isaac—she claims that her Head Costumer personality is taking over. "You have no *idea* how hot you're going to look in black eyeliner, darling," she says.

"No, I sure don't!" he agrees.

"Trust me," she says. "We'll meet you up at your room—wear that cute black button-down shirt and your baggy black jeans. You can be our Goth boy tonight."

I didn't bring anything even remotely formal looking with me. Katrina is delighted to discover this, because it means that she not only gets to do my makeup but dress me as well. She is obviously in her element.

"Battle, don't you think that Nic could fit into your jodhpurs?" she asks. We have converged in her room to get ready.

"Probably, yeah," says Battle.

"Well, go get your black ones. I have a plan."

Battle does. She comes back with both her black ones and her brown ones. She says, "I thought I could wear these," pointing to the brown ones, but Katrina shakes her head. "No, the concept here is to play up the whole butch-femme thing, only it'll be kind of reversed because of your hairstyles."

"Get over it, Katrina! Why don't you dress us like some of those wacky heterosexuals? I think they're *so* exotic and interesting," I say.

Katrina ignores me. "Nic, I see you with a Prince Valiant kind of look, while Battle here will be a postmodern Tinkerbell."

"I don't think so! Postmodern Tinkerbell, my ass."

I fall backwards into the orange beanbag chair, clapping my hands and cackling. "I *do* believe in fairies! I do! I do! I do believe in fairies!"

"Oh come on, just this once? Do it for me," Katrina pleads, batting her lashes.

"Hey, that may work on Isaac, but it won't fly with me, girlfriend." Battle shakes her head.

"You haven't even seen the dress!" Katrina says. She begins rummaging through her giant cardboard box of clothes, which she has continued to use in preference to actually storing her clothing in the closet or the dresser.

"Here it is!" she says triumphantly. The dress she's holding up is made of a fairly classy and subdued pale blue silk, but the bodice is outlined in purple sequins, and the skirt flares out at the bottom and is trimmed with a lavender feather boa.

"More mermaid than Tinkerbell," I comment from the beanbag chair. "Not worthy of Her Imperial Highness."

Battle smiles at me.

The day after we talked, she asked me if I still had the Empress. I said yes. She said, "Good." I didn't ask her to explain why she asked. The day after that, she said, "It must have taken you a long time to make that puppet." I nodded. On the third day, I set the Empress out on my dresser, and when Battle came to meet me for breakfast, she picked her up and put her into her backpack.

Neither of us has mentioned her since.

"It goes *perfectly* with your coloring," Katrina insists, holding the dress up to Battle. Battle looks down at the strapless dress with an expression that can only be described as long-suffering.

"Are you going to let her do this to me?" she asks me.

I just smile.

"Hey, when I'm done with her, it'll be your turn, baby," says Katrina.

"Yeah, but I like Prince Valiant," I say.

Battle sighs. "Never doubt that I love you," she says to Katrina, and takes her shirt and pants off, preparatory to putting the dress on.

I look away.

"Yay! Oh, I promise you won't regret this!" Katrina says, dancing around. "Let's see, you shouldn't need a bra under it, it ought to cinch you up pretty tight in there," she says, zipping Battle up in the back. "Perfect! Okay, now you, Nic—I want you both dressed before I do the makeup."

"Hey, what are *you* going to wear?" Battle demands.

Katrina looks down at herself. She's wearing an old World Wide Web Conference T-shirt and a ratty-looking pair of jeans. "I thought I'd go in costume as a programmer."

"Katrina Lansdale, you are going to wear something every bit as flamboyant as this or I am never going to speak to you again!" Battle crosses her arms over her sequin-covered chest and frowns.

"Kidding! I was kidding! I'll get dressed as soon as I'm done with you guys," Katrina promises.

After what seems like hours, but is really only about twenty minutes, Katrina has dressed me to her satisfaction. I'm wearing Battle's jodhpurs, which just barely fit me, with a voluminous purple silk Renaissance blouse and Battle's black leather boots. One of the early and delightful discoveries the three of us made was that we all wear the same size shoes.

"I feel like I should be stopping your carriage and demanding your jewels or your virtue," I say to Battle.

"What jewels?" Katrina asks.

"What virtue?" Battle asks.

"Okay, you have to close your eyes," says Katrina, with her hands inside the cardboard clothes box.

Battle and I close our eyes obediently. The sound of a zipper, fabric rustling, another zipper.

"Okay, open them!"

Katrina is wearing a green fifties taffeta dress with silver glitter squiggles, plastic skeleton earrings, and her purple combat boots. "Look, I'm Weetzie Bat!" she says.

"You don't have a bleached-blonde flattop," I point out. Katrina shrugs. "Battle does, so it's artistic license. And besides, I've got the right makeup."

"I feel like it's Halloween," Isaac complains as Katrina carefully blends his eyeliner. I think he'd be complaining more if it weren't for the fact that Katrina is straddling him as she works.

"You look so good!" Katrina says. "Doesn't he look great, guys?"

Isaac *does* look great. I've never seen him wear all black before. It does something for him. And the eyeliner, I have to admit, is a really nice touch. It makes him look a little dangerous, which is not Isaac's usual look at all. It almost makes me wish that kiss at the river had turned into something more. But not quite.

"You're gonna have to fend off the Angst Crows tonight," says Battle, slapping him on the back.

Isaac blushes. He reaches for his glasses, which Katrina took off and put on his computer desk. She grabs them before he can get them. "Nope, not tonight, babe. You have the rest of your life to be four-eyed."

"I can't goddamn see without them!" he says.

"Then I'll just have to lead you, honey," Katrina purrs.

Isaac doesn't have anything to say to that.

The dance is going to be in the auditorium. Apparently they can actually move out all those horrible uncomfortable chairs when the need arises.

"Somebody take a picture," says Isaac. He actually has a camera, unlike any of the rest of us.

Battle takes the camera and says "Sit on his lap, Katrina. That's perfect. Isaac, you're the Jewish James Dean."

"I'd rather be Lenny Bruce," says Isaac.

"But Lenny Bruce already *is* Jewish, so he can't be 'the Jewish Lenny Bruce.'" I point out.

"I'd still rather be Lenny Bruce. He dated a hot red-head, too, you know. She was a stripper!" Isaac leers.

Katrina blushes.

"Take a picture of us, too?" I ask Isaac.

"Sure," he says. Battle hands him the camera.

"I'll do one of you and Battle, but you need one of all three of you, too," he says.

"Wow, Isaac, that's really thoughtful," I say.

"What can I say, I'm just a sensitive New Age guy. Now put your hands on Battle like you're just about to cop a feel," says Isaac.

Battle and I shriek and refuse.

"All right, then just stand there holding hands and have a boring picture, see if I care."

Battle and I smile at each other, and Isaac takes the shot. Then he says, "Okay Katrina, you get on the end next to Nic. Nic, put an arm around both of them."

"That I can do," I say. We grin like fools, and Isaac snaps the picture.

"My god, I've died and returned to middle school," says Battle as the four of us survey the auditorium. Limp streamers and sad-looking balloons are festooned around at random intervals in the marginally transformed space. I say marginally transformed because the streamers and balloons and the lack of chairs are the only feeble stabs that have been made in the direction of decoration.

I shake my head. "So what I want to know is, how do they reconcile this with all those warnings that What's-His-Name gave us? Remember? 'Making romantic connections is not an appropriate use of your time here'?"

I was looking at Battle when he said that, I remember suddenly.

"Why, Nic, I'm surprised at you. You don't see any romance *here,* do you? This is just good clean drug-free fun, a nice change of pace for all our overtaxed genius brains," says Katrina.

"I think they're just hypocrites," says Battle.

The DJ is set up on the stage, in approximately the same position that Large Pink Bald Man was in when he gave his stunning speech. I can't identify the song that's playing now, but it features a drum machine and a syrupy female voice. There are a surprising number of people swaying around in vague time to it. I think I see Anne in the arms of some tall guy, and I feel pleased that she did manage to snag someone new.

"Did I ever tell you guys about Anne from Archaeology?" I ask. I give them the brief précis version of the saga of Anne and John, and explain my own advice to Anne to seek solace in the arms of another. "And there she is." I point to her. I think she's wearing the same dress that she was wearing in that Homecoming picture she showed me back at the beginning of the term.

"Dang!" says Battle.

"What?" I ask.

"Well, you know who that is with her, don't you?" she asks.

"No," I say.

"It's Kevin."

"Oh my god, you're right!"

For approximately five minutes, I can't even talk because I'm laughing too hard. Isaac and Katrina ignore me and actually dance to some random gushy number. Battle stands next to me, waiting for me to recover.

I take a deep breath, and say, "Okay, I'm all right now. That was just too funny. God, I don't want to have to talk to them, do you?" I ask.

"No way," says Battle. "We should, as they say, blow this Popsicle stand. Let me see if I can rouse the lovebirds."

She pokes Katrina and explains the situation. "Thank God—I hate this music," says Isaac. "And it's really hot wearing a long-sleeved shirt in this weather, *and* I can't see a goddamned thing."

"All right, we can leave. I just wanted one dance with you, my sweet," says Katrina.

We decide to walk to the river. Woods, river, courtyard: the big three destinations I will remember from this summer. I should have Isaac take pictures of them, too.

For a while, all four of us walk together, but Isaac and Katrina are slow. Katrina keeps finding flowers she wants to pick, and every time she stops to pick a flower, she and Isaac have to kiss again, and what with one thing and another, soon Battle and I have left them behind. My heart starts beating faster as soon as I realize this.

Battle and I have been holding hands on and off all evening, but that's all. We're close to the river now, and I say, "Want to sit down?" Battle nods. For a while, we just sit in silence, watching the river, watching the clouds and the stars in the sky.

"Look at the color of the sky right now," I say, speaking more softly than usual. "Doesn't it look like the way things look when you're remembering them? All soft and fuzzed out around the edges?"

Battle looks at me in the way she has that means I should either kiss her or keep talking, and I'm too scared to kiss her right now because maybe she doesn't really want me to. So I keep talking.

"What I'm saying is that it's like we're already gone. You're sitting in your room at home, thinking about this summer. I'm walking down the hall to class, and I bump into the wall, because I'm thinking about it, too. And this—"

I wave my hands to encompass the soft dark blue sky, the trees, the rock we're sitting on, the river, "—this is what it's going to look like in our minds."

"I'm going to miss you so much," Battle says.

"I can't even tell you how much I'm going to miss you," I answer. She reaches out for my hand, and I grab hers like a lifeline. We squeeze each other's hands so hard it makes us both laugh embarrassedly, and drop them.

"Eh, you think you're so tough," says Battle, rubbing the hand I grabbed with her other hand, as though to restore the circulation.

"Damn right," I say in my best tough-girl voice.

But not tough enough to stand losing you, Battle. Never that tough.

My eyes are going all blurry, and I know I'm going to cry again. I'm suddenly so furious that my voice comes out almost in a shriek when I demand, "How are we supposed to stand it? How the hell are we supposed to blithely pack our things and leave this place and pretend that everything is fine when we have to go back to the stupid, pointless, idiot, *moron* world again? It's not fair!"

Battle looks at me as though she might cry, too. Lighten up, Nic. I take a deep breath.

"Okay, I know—we'll just chat online all the time. We'll stop traffic on the Internet."

Battle smiles a little, and says, "Carrier pigeons."

"Singing telegrams. We'll raise them to an art form."

"Smoke signals . . ."

I lean my head on Battle's shoulder. "I want a happy ending, dammit."

Battle says, "It's not an ending. We're not even in college yet, for God's sake."

"Hey, there's an idea—we could go to the same school. All of us! You and me and Katrina and Isaac—"

"And Kevin?" Battle teases me.

"Screw Kevin. No, don't. Kevin can go to some nice music school a long way away from wherever we end up."

"It's a deal."

We shake hands solemnly. Then we look at each other. I'm struck by how ridiculous it is for us to be just shaking hands, after everything that's happened. Apparently she is too, because she suddenly puts her arms around me and starts kissing me, hard.

"They're probably wondering where we are," I say. The last thing I want to do is move right now, but we've abandoned Isaac and Katrina for quite some time. And it's getting a little cold out here.

Battle strokes my hair and laughs. "They're probably not either."

"Well, yeah, but where the heck would they be? I don't see Isaac being the type for a woodland frolic somehow, do you?" I ask. I sit up and reach out to retrieve my shirt, which has ended up several feet away from us.

Battle giggles. "I think he'd be the type for a frolic on nail-strewn concrete if it was with Katrina. Uh-oh—this dress is in pretty sad shape."

The postmodern Tinkerbell costume is severely grass-stained, and there are a lot of sequins missing from the bodice.

"I don't think she'll care," I say.

Battle giggles. "No, probably not. Zip me up?" she asks. I comply, pausing to kiss the back of her neck before I pull the zipper completely closed.

We link arms and start walking back toward Prucher Hall.

Ama me fideliter,
fidem meam nota:
de corde totaliter
et ex mente tota
sum presentialiter
absens in remota,
quisquis amat taliter,
volvitur in rota.

Love me faithfully! See how I am faithful: with all my heart and with all my soul, I am with you even when I am far away. Whosoever loves this much knows the torture of the wheel.

—from "Omnia sol temperat"
(The sun warms everything),
Carmina Burana, Cantiones Profanae

A Reader's Supplement to
Empress of the World . . .

FEATURING THREE STORIES BY SARA RYAN
ABOUT KATRINA, BATTLE, AND NIC:

"Me and Edith Head"
(illustrated by Steve Lieber)

"Click"
(illustrated by Dylan Meconis)

"Comparative Anatomy"
(illustrated by Natalie Nourigat)

Q and A with Sara Ryan

And more!

Me and Edith Head

Sara Ryan   Steve Lieber

Me and Edith Head

by Sara Ryan
art by Steve Lieber

I AUDITIONED TODAY FOR A MIDSUMMER NIGHT'S DREAM.

I WANT TO BE TITANIA, FALLING IN LOVE WITH A JACKASS IS WORTH IT IF YOU GET TO BE THE QUEEN OF THE FAIRIES.

YOU TOLD ME YOU PAID THE VISA BILL! OR DID YOU JUST SAY THAT SO YOU COULD GET OUT THE DOOR TO YOUR INFINITELY FASCINATING SOCIAL LIFE?

THERE'S NO NEED TO TAKE THAT TONE, JANET!

GETTING OUT OF THE HOUSE FOR REHEARSALS WOULD, OF COURSE, BE AN EXTRA BONUS.

CAST LIST

ST

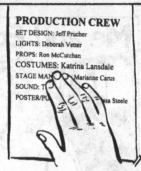

PRODUCTION CREW
SET DESIGN: Jeff Prucher
LIGHTS: Deborah Vetter
PROPS: Ron McCutchan
COSTUMES: Katrina Lansdale
STAGE MAN○○ Marianne Carus
SOUND: T
POSTER/PU ssa Steele

COSTUMES. ME. COSTUMES. IT'S LIKE MAKING BILL GATES YOUR INTERIOR DECORATOR.

I'M SUPPOSED TO MEET WITH YOU.

YOU MUST BE KATRINA, THEN.

LAST TIME I CHECKED.

WELCOME! LOOK AROUND! TRY ANYTHING YOU LIKE. IT'S A GOOD WAY TO GET TO KNOW WHAT WE HAVE.

IS THERE SOME KIND OF SYSTEM? SOME WAY THIS IS ORGANIZED?

NOT EXACTLY.

YOU HAVE TO CONSIDER OPTIONS, JUXTAPOSITIONS...

IN OTHER WORDS, IT'S COMPLETELY RANDOM.

WELL, ONCE YOU HAVE YOUR COSTUMES SET, YOU PUT THEM ASIDE.

WHAT DO YOU MEAN, ONCE YOU HAVE THEM **SET**? THEY DON'T EVEN HAVE ANY **SIZES** MARKED. HOW DO YOU KNOW IF THEY'RE GOING TO **FIT**?

THAT'S WHAT FITTINGS ARE FOR.

WHEN WE MADE A SKIRT IN HOME EC, I STITCHED MY THUMB TO THE HEM. IN MY HOUSE, CLOTHES ARE WHAT KEEP YOU FROM BEING ARRESTED FOR INDECENT EXPOSURE. THAT'S ALL. THIS IS ... SCARY.

AND THIS PLACE IS **INSANE.**

YOU'LL LEARN TO LOVE IT.

IS THAT WHAT HAPPENED TO YOU? THEY WOULDN'T CAST YOU, SO YOU STARTED DOING THIS INSTEAD?

NOT EXACTLY. COME WITH ME.

YOU DON'T HAVE TO BE ONSTAGE TO BE A STAR. TAKE THESE. READ THEM. LEARN FROM THEM.

EDITH HEAD? THAT'S LIKE THE WORST NAME EVER. DIDN'T PEOPLE MAKE FUN OF HER?

NOT AFTER SHE STARTED WINNING OSCARS.

3

"What you wear to keep that man happy and loving should be as carefully adhered to after marriage as before."

"With a home and children to care for, you can't always look as though you stepped out of a fashion advertisement, but you don't have to let him see you looking as though you were shot out of a cannon, either."

NOT EXACTLY A FEMINIST, WAS SHE?

I, ON THE OTHER HAND, BELIEVE IN EQUAL OPPORTUNITY.

ALL RIGHT, PROGRAMMERS. BEFORE WE RUN OUT OF TIME, WE'RE GOING TO TALK ABOUT YOUR FAVORITE SUBJECT—YOUR SEMESTER PROJECT.

USING WHAT YOU'VE LEARNED, EACH OF YOU IS GOING TO DESIGN A DATABASE. I DON'T CARE WHAT YOU PUT IN IT—YOUR CDs, YOUR COMIC BOOK COLLECTION, YOUR MISMATCHED SOCKS—

MR. ZAWINSKI?

DATAB

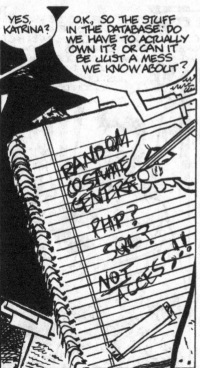

YES, KATRINA?

O.K., SO THE STUFF IN THE DATABASE: DO WE HAVE TO ACTUALLY OWN IT? OR CAN IT BE JUST A MESS WE KNOW ABOUT?

RANDOM COSTUME GENERA

PHP?

SQL?

NOT ACCESS!!

WELL, AS LONG AS YOU HAVE, UH, ACCESS TO THIS MESS

GREAT, PERFECT, THANKS!

R'NG

5

6

BECAUSE IT WOULD MAKE YOU LOOK BAD. YOU NEED TO SPIN THE VAPID STRAW UP THERE INTO GOLD. THAT'S YOUR JOB.

ARE YOU SUPPOSED TO TALK THAT WAY ABOUT FINE, UPSTANDING MEMBERS OF OUR STUDENT BODY?

SOMETIMES THE TRUTH HURTS.

THUMP.

SINCE THIS IS A MODERN-DRESS PRODUCTION, MOST OF YOU WILL BE WEARING YOUR OWN CLOTHES, BUT THE FAIRIES AND BOTTOM WILL BE COSTUMED. KATRINA LANSDALE WILL BE RESPONSIBLE FOR THAT.

KATRINA? WE'LL ALL LOOK LIKE WE SHOP AT GOODWILL.

DID I SAY FIVE? I MEANT FIFTY. FIFTY MILES OF BAD ROAD.

AUDITORIUM

REMEMBER THAT WE ARE ALL IN COSTUME, ALL THE TIME. AND WHEN YOU CHANGE YOUR COSTUME, YOU CHANGE THE WAY PEOPLE REACT TO YOU.

...VELVET SMOKING JACKET...

YOU MAY BE TREATED MORE, OR LESS, SERIOUSLY. PEOPLE YOU DO NOT LIKE OR RESPECT MAY BEGIN TO GIVE YOU COMPLIMENTS.

...WOMAN'S GRAY WOOL JODHPURS...

THEY'RE RESPONDING TO YOUR SURFACE. IT'S UP TO YOU TO DECIDE WHETHER TO GIVE ANY MORE THAN THAT.

...WOMAN'S SLEEVELESS TURTLENECK...

8

"...YOUR FATHER AND I HAVE DECIDED ..."

"...IT JUST ISN'T WORKING OUT..."

"...TRIED AS HARD AS WE..."

"...DIVORCE."

HERE... GO GET YOURSELF SOMETHING NICE.

"Accept the things you cannot change. Your liabilities may be turned into assets."

"Develop confidence in your appearance and dress to match that confidence."

13

SINCE THE FAIRIES ARE BOTH OLDER THAN THE HUMAN SOCIETY AND ALIEN TO IT, THEY SHOULD WEAR CLOTHES FROM A LONG TIME AGO THAT ALSO HAVE SOME ... UM ... SURREAL AND ALIEN ELEMENTS.

THINK OF IT AS THE INTERSECTION OF *GUYS AND DOLLS* AND GOTH.

OH, THAT'S GOOD. SHE'S GOOD.

WOW... WHERE DID YOU GET THAT OUTFIT?

THE GOODWILL.

...THINK BUT THIS, AND ALL IS MENDED...

WHEN SOMETHING RIPS APART-LIKE A DRESS, OR A FAMILY-SOMETIMES YOU CAN MEND IT.

OTHER TIMES YOU JUST HAVE TO TAKE THE PIECES AND MAKE THEM INTO SOMETHING NEW.

CLICK

SARA RYAN & DYLAN MECONIS

Comparative Anatomy

Sara Ryan   Natalie Nourigat

dear battle — i've been reading about comparative anatomy.

it makes me remember us.

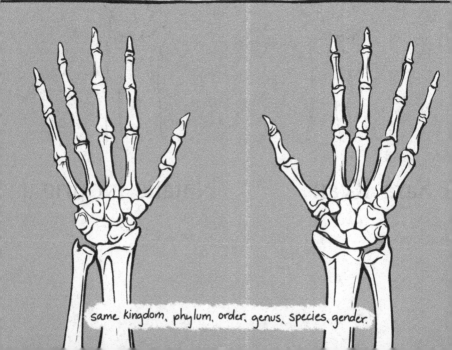

same kingdom, phylum, order, genus, species, gender.

i found your braid when i was moving. my ex wanted me to throw it out.

I'M ALWAYS COMPETING WITH YOUR PERFECT MAGICAL PAST!

WELL, SORRY I'M NOT HER!

i never said that sometimes i was sorry, too.

but it's not why i broke up with him.

not the only reason, anyway.

we have approved topics:

books!

movies!

music!

comics!

amusing and/or annoying friends and/or professors!

absent from list: us, love.

are you going? hat's safe to ask, right?

ot "are you happy?" ot "do you miss me?"

besides, i probably won't send this.

words still don't always work,

but i remain a fan of them.

so here are these: just to warn you, just a heads up.

if we're both there, at the reunion,

i might try to reunite.

Steve Lieber's comics and illustrations have been published by DC, Marvel, Dark Horse, Image, Dupuis, Scholastic, and many other publishers. His various projects have received nine Eisner Award nominations; and he won the Eisner for Best Limited Series for *Whiteout*, published by Oni Press. Steve's a founding member of Periscope Studio, the largest studio of comic book artists in North America. He lives in Portland, Oregon.

His Web site is **www.stevelieber.com**.

Dylan Meconis is a comics artist and writer. Her graphic novels include *Bite Me!* and *Family Man*. She has also collaborated with Sara on "Fair Trade," the only comics story in the *Welcome to Bordertown* anthology. She is jealous of Sara's shoe collection.

Find her work at **www.dylanmeconis.com**.

Natalie Nourigat works out of Periscope Studio in Portland, Oregon, as a freelance artist. She is currently drawing graphic novels for Oni Press, Image Comics, and Lerner Publishing Group. She takes French and karate and loves to travel.

Her work can be seen at **www.natalienourigat.com**.

On *Empress of the World*

How did the publication of *Empress* affect your life?

I think for any author, when your first book is published, it splits your life into Before and After. Your aspirations shift, and your anxieties do, too. People can pick up this book you've put years of your life into, read it in a few hours, and then wonder when your next one is coming. Suddenly you start getting this sense of an audience, and if you're not careful you can tie yourself in knots worrying about what that audience wants and expects from you.

I've heard from a *lot* of readers that *Empress* was the first book they ever read about two girls in love. (I still hear this, more than ten years later.) I've gotten so many heartfelt emails that I'm honored to have received; from readers in love, from readers struggling after a breakup, from readers who told me they understood themselves a little better after reading the book. And yes, sometimes when I was working on [the companion novel] *The Rules for Hearts*, I *did* tie myself in knots, wanting to write another book that would affect readers in exactly the same way. Finally I figured out that's not possible. Every book is different, and readers change, too. I'm absolutely grateful for and appreciative of my readers—you all are fabulous and amazing! But now, when I'm writing, I try very hard to pretend you don't exist.

Talk a little bit about the companion book to *Empress*: *The Rules for Hearts*. (Note: The prologue and first chapter follow this section.)

After I wrote *Empress of the World*, I knew that Battle Hall Davies needed her own voice. In *Empress*, we only see her through her girlfriend's eyes: beautiful, compelling, ultimately inexplicable. But of course, that's not how Battle sees herself.

I also knew that Battle's brother meant a lot to her. I wanted to see how he compared to the vision of him she built up in his absence from her life.

I grew up in Ann Arbor, Michigan, and I was always fascinated by college students. I'd go to old movies on campus sponsored by the Student Film Society and watch the audience as much as the screen. I eavesdropped on their conversations, I read their buttons and T-shirt slogans, and I tried to project myself forward in time.

At fourteen, I got my wish. I started hanging out with college students, and with people who were even older. Working for a summer theater festival gave me a multigenerational peer group. When I started writing *The Rules for Hearts*, I remembered how I felt then, like what I was really auditioning for was the role of myself, grown up.

On LGBTQI Issues

How has the world changed for LGBTQI teens since the publication of *Empress*?

In some ways, it's changed fairly dramatically. There are (a few) more mainstream representations of queer folks in the media. There are more gay-straight alliances in schools. There are high-visibility national projects supporting queer youth, like It Gets Better (www.itgetsbetter.org), and youth activism efforts, like Make It Better (makeitbetterproject.org). There are some places where you can legally marry your same-gender partner.

On the other hand, there's still a very strong *need* for projects such as It Gets Better and Make It Better. There are still a lot of communities where it's very hard to come out and be out. Yeah, you can get information and support and connect with other queer youth online. But if you don't have easy access—you share a computer with family members whom you're not out to, or you can only get online at school or the library or only by using your old, slow phone—then it can be really challenging to feel like you're not alone.

But there has been a generational shift in attitudes, and that suggests that we may see more positive change. In 2011, according to the Millennials, Religion, & Gay and Lesbian Issues Survey carried out by Public Religion Research, more than six out of ten 18–29-year-olds support same-gender marriage, 69% favor same-sex couples jointly adopting children, 71% support civil unions, and 79% back LGBT-inclusive employment nondiscrimination legislation. So while there's clearly still a long way to go, there has been significant progress.

On Writing

Why must you write? What would you do if you weren't a writer? (Or, What was the best job you had before becoming an author?)

Even if I'm between projects, I see the world through a writer's lens, analyzing my experiences for future use. This past summer, traveling alone, late at night, I fell and hurt myself. I was upset and in pain, but I was also thinking. *Right, when people are tired they're more prone to injury. And fatigue escalates emotions. So in that scene when X loses it, he should also hurt himself.* I iced my sprained finger, then started making notes.

So I can't imagine not writing. That said, like many writers, I have a day job, and it is a fabulous one: I work as a librarian.

How do you manage to combine being a librarian and a writer?

1. *Always, always carry a notebook.* You can't control when you'll have an idea for a new project or suddenly see how to solve a problem in a manuscript, so make sure you've always got a place to jot down some notes. I've gotten better about this over the years. Very occasionally I still have to resort to cryptic scribbling on a receipt or the back of a meeting agenda (ahem), but usually I'm prepared.

I also think it's important for this notebook to be *dedicated* to writing projects and not used for anything else. Here's why. Let's say you've decided you'll put all your writing notes in your personal journal, because after all, you are a fully integrated person and you can't, you know, compartmentalize yourself, man, your writing comes from your HEART, and your HEART is in your journal.

So you flip open your journal to note down what you've just realized needs to happen right after the sword fight scene, and the first thing you see is the intricate dissection of a recent relationship drama, or the nearly illegible, yet compelling, evidence of your latest middle-of-the-night gnawing anxiety attack—and before you know it, that idea is gone. I am all for keeping a journal, too—but in the immortal words of the Offspring, you gotta keep 'em separated.

2. *Have work dates.* Work dates with friends who are also writers allow for simultaneous social interaction and productivity! The key to this strategy, of course, is to keep the former from overwhelming the latter. My best work dates happen when we go to a coffee shop and agree to declare a break at a specified time, like, say, a half hour or forty-five minutes after we begin. Then we talk for maybe ten minutes, maybe as long as fifteen, then put our heads down again and work for another half hour, forty-five minutes. Repeat until everyone's too jittery to work more, or our energy has given out, or some combination.

3. *Between jobs, rest and "reboot."* I don't do this every day, but I find that if I've had a challenging day at work and I know I need to do a lot of writing in the evening, it helps to take a short nap, or at least lie down and close my eyes, before I open my laptop. In extreme cases I will try to fool myself into thinking that I'm starting an entirely new day by showering after my nap. And then drinking some coffee. Which tends to lead to rapidly accumulating sleep dep, but, um, well. It's something I do.

4. *Write short pieces as well as long ones.* As my patient readers know, I am not the fastest gun in the Pacific Northwest. Doing shorter pieces means not only that folks will have things to read from me between novels but also that *I* get the satisfaction that comes from completing a project. When I'm working on a novel, it's impossible for me to judge how long it will take. At some point early in the novel-writing process, I always think the equivalent of the optimistic generals at the beginning of the First World War: "Ah, it'll all be over by Christmas." And then I find myself in a trench wearing an ill-fitting gas mask and dodging shrapnel, and it seems impossible that I'll make it out alive. It is an extremely good idea, when you're in that trench, to climb out and write something that you can *finish.* This even works, on a smaller scale, with blog posts.

5. *Don't beat yourself up.* This is one of those do-as-I-say-not-as-I-do pieces of advice. I am constantly aware that my friends who don't have day jobs are publishing more frequently. I am constantly worried that I'm not fast enough, that people will forget me between books, that I'm not getting enough done. BUT. I try to remember: I care about *both* careers. My work as a librarian is rewarding, too. And publishing is not a race.

How is writing fiction different from writing a graphic novel?
Ways in which the process is similar:
- I spend a lot of time staring into the middle distance, trying to figure out if that character would actually do X, say Y, or react in Z fashion.
- I scrutinize my notes.
- Every so often when I'm doing something that I think is entirely unrelated to the story, such as watching a movie or attempting to fall asleep, an idea will bubble up to the surface that I'm imme-

diately compelled to scribble down because it fixes a problem or provides an insight into an aspect of a character's arc that was previously opaque.

- I print pages and cross out things, then scrawl the new text in the margins and on the back of the paper. There is something about the physicality of actual handwriting that seems to work better than endlessly deleting and retyping on the computer. I don't know why.

- I waste time on the Internet, feel guilty, and eventually turn on MacFreedom so I can get some damn work done.

Ways in which writing a graphic novel is different:

- I need to make more choices per scene. The process is not simply about determining what happens to which characters and how to transition between different parts of the story. It's about how the reader will see it all play out on the page. A tight focus on the characters, for nuances of expressions and body language? Tiny silhouettes against a complex and crowded background? Characters entirely absent, replaced by images that function as counterpoint to narrative text? The details of these choices will, of course, be worked out by my artist—and that's a fundamental difference between the two mediums for me. I can't draw, so my short comics and graphic novels will always be collaborations. Because of that, I'm trying to teach myself to err on the side of providing maximum information in my panel descriptions about the mood I want to evoke.

- I draw (a few incredibly poorly rendered) thumbnails to help make sure I'm asking for something that makes sense visually. (I also bite my thumbnails, and the ones on my other fingers, too. But that is a way in which working on a script is the same as working on prose.)

IF YOU LIKE THAT SORT OF THING, IT'S THE SORT OF THING YOU'D LIKE

A SUGGESTED BOOK LIST

More than a decade after *Empress* first appeared, there still aren't a tremendous number of young adult books with queer girl protagonists, and they're surprisingly elusive in graphic novels, too. I've included some older titles, some that were published for adults, and a few without queer girl protagonists but with other elements that might resonate.

***Skim* by Mariko and Jillian Tamaki** (Groundwood). Mariko's writing is heartfelt and often hilarious. Jillian's drawing is elegant. Any story that includes a torturous teacher crush, awkward school assemblies, Wicca, goths, and sarcastic journal entries is most definitely relevant to my interests.

***My Heartbeat* by Garret Freymann-Weyr** (Houghton Mifflin Harcourt). Ellen wants to understand the relationship between her brother, Link, and his best friend, James. It's complicated, especially because Ellen is *totally, madly in love* with James. Are they gay? What does it even mean to be gay? I most appreciate how smart Freymann-Weyr's characters are and how Ellen's practical approach to self-education collides with her intense feelings.

***Hey, Dollface* by Deborah Hautzig** (Marshall Cavendish). This book was first published in 1978, making it effectively a historical novel for contemporary readers. Chloe and Val, both aspiring painters, find each other at a girls' school where everyone else seems rich, placid, and complacent. Their complicated friendship develops against the backdrop of seventies New York City after the first wave of gay liberation. Val's voice as a narrator, a mix of sophisticated and naive, beautifully conveys what it feels like to be questioning—and questioning everything, not just sexuality.

***The Bermudez Triangle* by Maureen Johnson** (Razorbill/Penguin). Nina, Avery, and Mel have been inseparable best friends since they were five. The summer before their senior year of high school, Nina goes to a leadership institute and falls in love with Steve from Oregon, while Avery and Mel work at the heinous, faux-Irish P.J. Mortimer's in the mall. When Nina returns, Avery and Mel are together. The point of view shifts between the three girls throughout the book, giving the reader multiple perspectives on how their relationships shift as well. Funny, sweet, smart, and genuine.

Kissing Kate by **Lauren Myracle** (Speak/Penguin). When Lissa and her best friend, Kate, kiss at a party, it changes everything, but not in the way a reader might hope it would. The way Lissa copes with the awkwardness between her and Kate is utterly real. Lissa's family and the working-class Atlanta community ring true, too: her uncle Jerry, who's raised her since her parents died; her little sister, Beth, who wants to be older than fifth grade; Darlin, the caterer she works for and Kimberly, whose spiritual name is Ariel, who convinces Lissa to try things she never would have done on her own.

A Love Story Starring My Dead Best Friend by **Emily Horner** (Dial/Penguin). This book is about putting on a musical called *Totally Sweet Ninja Death Squad*. It's also about a solo bike ride across the country. And dealing with grief. And figuring out who your friends are. And yeah, it's a love story, too; and it pulls you in from the first sentence: "Dear Julia, I'm writing this because I still turn around whenever I hear your name, and I just turned around."

grl2grl by **Julie Anne Peters** (Little, Brown). Peters doesn't linger in any of these stories, some so short they're more like fragments. She zooms in on intense moments: mustering the courage to attend a gay-straight alliance meeting, suffering assault at the hands of bigots, struggling after a breakup, declaring love. (The author is serializing a companion volume, *grl2grl2*, online.)

The Lover's Dictionary by **David Levithan** (Farrar, Straus, & Giroux). This concise, elegant novel, my favorite so far of Levithan's always notable books, is in the form of dictionary definitions. Each entry is complete in itself but simultaneously contributes to the larger story. Levithan doesn't specify the lovers' genders, and that adds to the book's inviting quality.

Locas and ***Locas II*, the Maggie and Hopey Stories by Jaime Hernandez** (Fantagraphics). These gigantic, gorgeous graphic novels collect the *Love and Rockets* stories that focus on Maggie Chascarillo and Esperanza Glass, mostly known as Hopey. Maggie and Hopey meet as underage California punks and become lovers shortly thereafter. The nature of their relationship keeps shifting throughout their adventures together and apart, but they remain important in each other's lives. I love these characters; I love the way Jaime draws them and their world, with never a wasted brushstroke or superfluous panel.

Anything and everything by Alison Bechdel. When I was a nervous, newly out queer girl in the early nineties, *Dykes to Watch Out For* was my field guide to a particular lesbian subculture—based in a college town, with drama unfolding in food co-ops, political protests, group houses, classrooms, vegetarian restaurants, and, of course, the women's bookstore: Madwimmin Books. I've loved watching Bechdel's art and storytelling evolve over the years. When her graphic memoir, *Fun Home: A Family Tragicomic* (Houghton Mifflin Harcourt), became such a success, I felt an almost proprietary pride.

***Portland Queer*, edited by Ariel Gore** (Lit Star Press). I live in Portland. In these first-person narratives, I recognize streets, bars, cafés, schools, even bicycles. But you don't have to live where I live to appreciate this eclectic collection, peopled with Catholic schoolgirls, a gay waiter crushed out on a straight one, a devoted MMORG player, a pregnant man in love with a bearded lady, lesbian landscapers, and many other queers of note.

***Tam Lin* by Pamela Dean** (Firebird/Penguin). It would require extra-dimensional time-travel, but I think that if Nicola Lancaster met Janet Carter, they would enjoy each other's company. *Tam Lin* takes place at a small Midwestern liberal arts college in the early seventies. Professor's daughter Janet makes friends; copes with roommate drama; engages deeply with literature, theater, and certain actors; and struggles with a slowly growing sense that there's more going on in the Classics department than scholarly research.

***Fair Play* by Tove Jansson** (New York Review Books). I grew up with Jansson's Moomin books and was delighted when I found this. It's connected stories about a couple, Jonna and Mari, as they accommodate and resist each other's idiosyncrasies, and navigate their days and lives together and separately. Jonna is an artist and filmmaker, Mari a writer and illustrator, so the stories are also about creative work and the ways they both support and resent each other's art.

The Necessary Hunger by **Nina Revoyr** (St. Martin's). Nancy Takahiro's dad falls in love with Raina Webber's mom at a basketball game. Nancy's already half in love herself, with Raina. Raina and her mom move in with Nancy and her dad just as the girls' senior year of high school begins. I love this book's L.A. setting, the diverse cast, how much sports matter to both girls, and the matter-of-fact way Revoyr writes about their sexuality.

And Now We Are Going to Have a Party: Liner Notes to a Writer's Early Life by **Nicola Griffith** (Payseur & Schmidt). Reading this memoir is like opening a box of presents; and I mean that literally, because it's packaged in a box, with postcards, chapbooks, a poster, and even a CD. I can't say it better than Dorothy Allison does in her preface: "This is a map of the changing world, the world that changed as Nicola became the writer she is, and the world we all share that has changed as so many women and queers and deeply unique outlaw voices began to speak all the stories not told before."

Zami: A New Spelling of My Name by **Audre Lorde** (Crossing Press). This book is sort of a memoir. Lorde herself invented a word to describe its genre: *biomythography*. She writes about growing up in New York in the forties and fifties, living in Mexico in a radical expatriate community during the McCarthy era; about being smart and black and lesbian; about friends and lovers, politics and jobs. Her prose is both precise and poetic—which makes sense since she's also distinguished for her poetry. Reading *Zami* feels very intimate; it's a privilege to experience her world.

Some Musicians I Might or Might Not Have Been Listening to at Various Moments During the Era in Which I Was Writing *Empress of the World*

A Playlist

Coming up with this playlist necessitated an archaeological dig of sorts.

I started writing about Nic in 1997, two years out of grad school, about to move from Ann Arbor, where I grew up and went to school, to Portland, which has been home ever since. A significant percentage of my music still came from mix tapes. Like, actual cassette tapes, not the online versions that people make now. The tapes are lost to history, but I remember tracks. The CDs live in notebooks now; the cases were discarded years ago. I flipped through the notebooks with many exclamations about albums I'd forgotten and made a stack to burn. Based on the available evidence, here are some artists I was probably listening to while I wrote *Empress*.

Ani diFranco. I'm sure there were any number of queer girls in the nineties who *weren't* listening to Ani, but I have not met many of them. Fiercely intricate guitar, sometimes sweet, sometimes blunt, but always smart lyrics. And if you want a bisexual anthem, look no farther than "In Or Out," from her album *Imperfectly*.

Sloan. Early in our acquaintance, my esteemed editor Sharyn introduced me to Sloan, and I was hooked from the first line of "Underwhelmed": *She was underwhelmed, if that's a word.* The music has so much energy; the lyrics are sharp and often funny.

Voice of the Beehive. A friend put one of VOTB's songs on a mix tape that I played until it disintegrated, and that song "I Say Nothing" is still a favorite, perhaps in part because of the incongruous but memorable line *All those endless days of all those sci-fi slaves*. And I love the contrast between their cheery, bouncy sound and the bitter quality of many of their lyrics.

Tom Waits. I've been listening to Tom Waits [for approximately ever.] I remember a housemate complaining that he sounded like a dwarven dirge, which only made me want to play his music even more often. I also recommend reading interviews with him; he has worthwhile things to say about creativity.

The Story. Another band I was introduced to via a track on a mix tape; in this case it was "The Alarm Is on Love" from *Grace in Gravity*. Jonatha Brooke's and Jennifer Kimball's voices are so gorgeous together. And on what other album can you find songs inspired by both Gary Larson and E. E. Cummings?

Veda Hille. In "Me and Edith Head," Katrina wears a T-shirt that's a homage to the first Veda Hille album I bought, *Spine*. I've seen Veda perform multiple times, and I always get all shivery and fangirlish. The bio on her Web site contains the sentence "Childhood interests included plants, books, microscopes, science fiction, and psychiatry," which gives you an idea of what influences her eclectic and brilliant songs.

Kruder & Dorfmeister. As is evident from the artists I've mentioned so far, I love smart lyrics. But lyrics can be distracting when I write, so sometimes I look instead for music that's more concerned with interesting rhythms that will occupy a different slice of my brain. You can put Kruder & Dorfmeister's remixes on as background; the mood will still seep in.

Looper, *Geometrid*. The vocals from this Scottish band are whispery and sweet, and there's often a lot of repetition in the lyrics, which gives the songs a hypnotic quality. The songs are about things such as trying to drive while lots of bugs are hitting your windshield ("Bug Rain"), changing or perhaps not changing your coiffure ("Money Hair"), and being hopeful and defiant in the face of potential technological crisis ("Y2K Song").

Little Sue. I started listening to this band because my then-violin teacher was performing with them. Gorgeous, plaintive, bittersweet.

Tricky, *Maxinquaye*. The word for Tricky's and Martina Topley-Bird's vocals on this album is *insinuating*. *Smoky* might fit, too. It's an album that calls for dim light and not being in a hurry to get anywhere.

Carmina Burana as recorded by the San Francisco Symphony, conducted by Herbert Blomstedt. Years before I began to write *Empress*, I was in a chorus that performed *Carmina Burana*, and the experience stuck with me. If you've been to any costume-y huzzah-type action movies, you've probably heard the superepic "O Fortuna"; it's a frequent soundtrack choice. I recommend the rest of the cycle, too.

A peek at the companion to
Empress of the World . . .

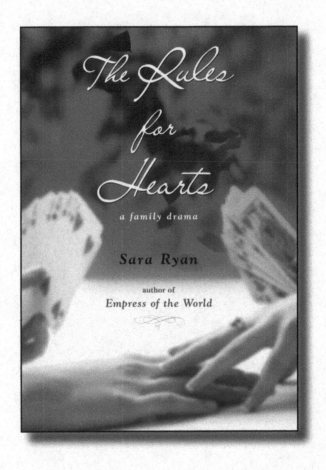

The Rules
for
Hearts

a family drama

Sara Ryan

author of
Empress of the World

PROLOGUE

Church basement, Chapel Hill, North Carolina, almost five years ago

IT'S BINGO NIGHT. My brother, Nick, and I are in the youth room next to the social hall, playing hearts. We always play hearts on bingo night.

Dad used to be an actor, so he never needs a microphone, whether he's preaching or calling the numbers. We hear him boom, "O-69!"

We crack up.

Nick is sixteen, I'm thirteen, and he's my favorite person. He's smarter and funnier and more charming than anyone. He teaches me card tricks and dirty jokes. He says that everyone except me is a hypocrite, especially Mom and Dad. He knows the best music, the best places to go, and he hardly ever complains about his tagalong little sister.

Three weeks later, on his seventeenth birthday, he runs away.

ACT I

Are You Lost?

scene i

IT'S MY FOURTH time around this block. I'm idling—again—in front of an old purple house, almost invisible behind a tall, ivy-covered fence.

A dark-haired girl opens the gate, walks up to my car, and taps on my window.

"Are you lost?" she asks.

I roll down the window and hand the girl a piece of paper.

"I'm looking for this address."

"You've found it. You must be Nick's sister, right?"

I nod, pull over, and park. My hands are shaking. I have pictured the end of this trip since I pulled out of Mom and Dad's driveway six days ago, but the scenes in my head never included anyone but me and my brother.

I rub my eyes, rake my hands through what there is of my hair, open the car door, and get out.

"I'm Meryl," the dark-haired girl says. She holds out her hand. "One of the housemates."

"Battle," I say.

Meryl's curly black hair is escaping from a low ponytail tied with a bright orange ribbon. Her white T-shirt is snug under her faded green overalls, and I can see the muscles in her shoulders. When I take her hand, I feel a jolt I haven't felt in more than a year.

Uh-oh. I didn't picture this scene, either.

"I'll help you unload," Meryl says.

"Thank you. Um, do you happen to know where my brother is?"

It feels funny to say "my brother." It's not a phrase I've had much occasion to use for a while.

"Nope, no idea. Let's get your stuff onto the porch."

"Thanks, but I need to make a quick call first."

I'm dizzy with fatigue, but Mom and Dad need to hear that I've arrived safely.

They know I'm moving into a house with some people for the summer before I start at Reed College. I showed them the ad on the Internet.

They don't know that one of the people is their son.

I dial, the phone rings, the machine picks up. "Hey,

I'm here, I'm fine, I'll talk to you soon." I hang up.

The air feels soft. The sky is gray, with a few thin clouds, and something about the quality of the light makes the green of leaves and grass seem brighter.

"Okay, I've done my duty. Let me open the trunk," I say.

Meryl and I each grab a box. Meryl reads, "'Paperbacks, white bookshelf.' God, color-coordinated labels? *Sure* you're related to Nick?"

I smile. "It's just easier. You know."

"No"—Meryl shakes her head—"*easy* is when you throw everything into the back of the truck, floor it, and get the hell out of Dodge."

"I wouldn't know about that," I say.

But Nick would.

Meryl and I walk back and forth from the car to the porch, piling up boxes. My eyes swim and my balance is a little off, but I don't say anything. It's not Meryl's fault that my brother can't be bothered to meet me, when it's been four and a half years since I've seen him and I've driven across the country to move in with him.

Then I pick up one of the few boxes I've labeled FRAGILE, get halfway up the walk, and trip.

The box flies out of my hands, hits the ground, and opens. Styrofoam packing peanuts spill out, along with what they're protecting: two puppets, a boy and a girl. Some of them broke the girl's fall. But the boy landed right on the concrete walk.

"Are you okay?" Meryl asks.

"Fine." I squat to pick up the peanuts before the breeze sends them all over the neighborhood.

Meryl kneels to investigate the boy.

The little gold crown he'd worn has split in half.

"Hmm, this is kind of broken," she says.

"I think I'll be able to fix it." I nestle the puppets back into the box, then pick up the halves of the boy's crown.

They look like a charm, but for what?

I put the crown halves into the pocket of my hoodie, then pick up another box.

Once we've gotten everything out of my car, Meryl says, "Take the stereo faceplate, too. Or at least put it in the glove compartment."

"Okay." This doesn't look like a bad neighborhood. What am I not seeing?

I shove the faceplate into the glove compartment, on top of the trip planner that's gotten me from Chapel Hill to Portland.

"Smoke break," Meryl says, digging into the pocket of her overalls and retrieving a pack and a lighter.

"Don't worry, nobody smokes in the house," she adds, grinning to reveal small, crooked, slightly yellow teeth.

While Meryl smokes, I take a closer look at the purple house I'm moving into. It's old—Victorian maybe?—and huge, with lots of windows that have that ripply-looking glass.

Nick didn't even tell me how many people live here, just that I'd like them.

Where is he?

"So how long did it take you to get here?" Meryl asks.

"About a week. It would've been faster, but I stayed in hotels for a couple of nights."

"Swank."

I shake my head. "More like antiswank. This one place had a patch of fluorescent orange mold growing on the carpet."

"Ew, and you *stayed* there? I'd have left."

A cab screeches to a stop in front of the house. My pulse thuds in my throat. Nick drives a cab now, he told me.

"That's probably him now," Meryl says.

But it's a woman who steps out. She's about my mom's age, and it looks like she spends a lot of time on her eyebrows. They're perfectly arched. Her black hair is growing out, though—I see about an inch of gray roots.

She stomps up the porch steps. "I need nicotine."

She takes two cigarettes from Meryl's pack, puts one in her mouth, cups the other in her palm like a tiny doll. "Flame," she demands. Meryl leans in with her lighter.

"Oh, God," the woman says. "This day. This goddamn *day*. What is all this?"

She waves at my stuff, then notices me.

"Oh! Excuse me, you must be—what did Nick tell me your name was?"

"Battle."

"*Excellent.* A fierce name. We need more of those. Battle, I'm Aurora—*not* a fierce name, alas."

"But you make up for it," Meryl says.

"*Thank* you. Anyway, Battle, I'm Aurora, and I own this place. Welcome to Forest House."

"Thanks."

"If I were a good person, I'd help you move everything up into your room, but frankly, after the day I've had, the very *idea* exhausts me, so my proposal is that we wait for your lovely brother to turn up and make him do it."

"Okay. Can you tell me where a restroom is?"

"Past the kitchen on the left."

As soon as I step inside, I see why Aurora calls it Forest House. There are more plants here than I've ever seen inside a building, in pots, in hanging baskets, in planters—from African violets like the ones Grandma always had to rubber trees with branches that graze the ceiling. Jungle House would be more accurate.

Though a jungle wouldn't have so many books. Some are stacked on brick-and-board shelves, some are in teetery piles on the floor. It looks and smells like a greenhouse crossed with a used bookstore.

There are even plants growing inside the dirt-filled claw-foot tub. God, I hope there's another bathroom upstairs, and it's not that everyone in the house is opposed to bathing.

When I get back out to the porch, Aurora's in the middle of a sentence:

"—all over the damned play! Lovers and madmen. Love in idleness. The course of true love. Love love love love love. Blah blah blah, et cetera, et cetera."

Aurora looks up. "Battle! *You'll* bring a fresh perspective! Tell me: should I get married?"

"Um . . . to whom?"

"Mister Robert Cracknell. You'll meet him soon; he lives here, too. I hope that doesn't shock you."

"It doesn't." If anything, I'm shocked that she's asking my opinion after having known me for less than fifteen minutes.

"Good, because if it did, I'm sure you'd be far *more* shocked by . . . hmmm . . . well, never mind, you'll meet everyone soon enough. *Anyway*, Robert has asked me to marry him. I can't imagine how he could have even *thought* of asking me when he *knows* we're about to start *Midsummer*!"

"Hey, the show's all about the weddings," Meryl says.

Aurora sighs. "It is, and it isn't. It's really a lot about hierarchies, and overturning them—and how you don't come out of the forest unchanged—but it *is* about love and marriage, too, certainly. So I think it was very manipulative of him to make this . . . *proposition* just now. Don't you think so, Battle?"

"I couldn't say."

Where the hell is Nick?

"It's really the *idea* of marriage, how it shuts off all kinds of options, the idea of giving up forever those very first moments you have with someone new, before you've even kissed, when you just get that *connection*—"

Meryl grabs my hands and stares dreamily into my eyes. Aurora laughs and says, "Yes, exactly! When you're oblivious to the world, just absorbed in each other."

The way Meryl's hands feel almost takes my mind off my brother. I can't meet her eyes.

Meryl doesn't let go, and Aurora goes on, in an even softer, sweeter voice, "But you're not sure yet, you can't take anything for granted, I mean, what if you've misinterpreted all those signs you thought you saw? You can't know, until somebody makes that first move. . . ."

I feel hypnotized. I lean closer. Meryl leans toward me, too.

My brain isn't working. It's not telling me that it's crazy to be millimeters away from kissing a strange girl because an even stranger woman says she misses what it feels like to have a crush.

"Well, no introductions necessary, I see," my brother says.

The spell is broken. Meryl and I move away from each other, and I look up.

"Your hair's longer than mine," I say stupidly. "And you have earrings."

He's smiling. His face is thinner. He's got what looks like a three-day growth of beard, and there's something different about his eyes; they seem—what? Not tired. Not bloodshot.

Older?

"I can't believe you're really here!" he says. "God, when'd you get so tall?"

I haven't stopped being angry. "Sometime in the past four and a half years."

He crushes me into a hug, and after a frozen second, I put my arms around him and hug him back.

"Are you guys twins?" Meryl asks. "You look alike."

A strangled sound, not quite a laugh, not quite a cough, comes out of my throat.

Nick says, "Sure."

"No, we're not." I step out of the hug. "Nick, I have a present for you."

The last few weeks before I left, I went all over Chapel Hill taking pictures of everywhere we used to go together. Some things had changed, of course, but I figured he'd want to know that, too.

I find the box labeled MEMENTOS, ETC., open it, and take out the album. I used archival paper and acid-free photo corners. The cover is dark forest green, his favorite color. Or at least it used to be.

"Here," I say.

Nick opens it, flips quickly from page to page, a slight, vague smile on his face.

It's only then that it occurs to me that making a scrapbook of the place my brother ran away from was not, perhaps, my most brilliant idea ever.

"You spent a lot of time on that," he says. "I can tell."

Then he sets the album down and reaches into a paper bag.

"Got a present for you, too."

He hands me a six-pack of Pabst, smiling the way he always used to when he'd give me a Coke that he'd shaken up.

I pull out a can, pop the top. The beer geysers up out of the can, spilling over my hands and arms. Nick laughs and applauds.

"He's always doing that. I thought you'd have known," Meryl says.

"Oh, *thanks!*" I say. I grab for Nick and make sure to wet his jacket and T-shirt while I hug him again, inhaling the malty scent of beer.

"You're welcome," he says. Getting dampened with beer doesn't appear to bother him.

I raise my can to him and take a sip.

"Y'all should have some, too," I say. "Though you might want to let it sit a minute."

Aurora, Meryl, and Nick all take cans.

A stocky, bearded man pushes open the gate, walks up the steps, and glares at us. He looks at Aurora. "Enjoying yourself?"

"Robert, this is our new housemate, Nick's sister. Her name is Battle."

The man shifts his glare to me. "Hello, Battle. If I were you, I'd get my crap off the porch before I started partying. But"—he sniffs the air, wrinkles his nose—"I guess it's a little late for that. If you'll excuse me."

He goes past us into the house.

What a great first impression. Thanks, Nick.

Meryl whistles. "Stay out of *his* way. Go be nice to him, Aurora."

Aurora says, "I most certainly will *not*. He was extremely rude. Battle, I must apologize on his behalf."

I set down the beer. "Will someone show me where my room is?"

"Absolutely," says my brother. "And we'll all help carry up the boxes, right?" He smiles at Aurora and Meryl.

"You don't have to," I say. "I can do it."

"No worries," says Meryl. "You don't have that much stuff. We can bucket-brigade it."

And that's what we do—each box goes from Aurora on the porch, to Meryl in the middle of the living room, to me at the foot of the stairs, to Nick at the doorway of my new room. Despite the supposed efficiency, I'm the only one running up and down the stairs, but I don't mind. I've been on the road for days, and my legs welcome the work.

Once Meryl has passed the last box (HARDBACKS) to me, she and Aurora disappear, and I carry it up the stairs to the door where Nick's waiting. I'm sweating a little and breathing fast.

"Behold!" Nick says, pushing the door open with one foot. My new room is small, with freshly painted white walls, a scuffed, scratched dark wood floor, and a tiny closet with nothing in it but three empty hangers and a blue baseball cap hanging from a nail. The room has one big open window that looks out onto the back garden. I set down the last box. My arms feel a little rubbery, in that way that happens when you're suddenly no longer carrying something heavy.

I sit on the windowsill and, holding on with one hand, lean backward out of the window, feeling the slight breeze move through my hair.

"Nice view, huh?" Nick says.

"Yeah," I say, halfway upside down. I see that Meryl and Aurora are in the backyard, talking and gesturing with their cigarettes, too far away for me to hear.

"Glad you're here," Nick says. "I wasn't sure you were going to make it."

"Why not?"

"Parental controls."

I laugh. I had to learn how to disable those back when I started IMing, and somewhere along the line, I'd turned the phrase into shorthand for every form of discipline Mom and Dad imposed.

I pull myself upright. "It wasn't a big deal," I lie. "I said I wanted to get to know the area before school started, the end. It's not like I said, 'Oh, by the way, last year Nick tracked me down on the Internet and told me I should go to Reed, and that's why I chose that school, and now I'm moving in with him for the summer.' As far as they know, you're still in New York working on that show or whatever you said on the postcard. That was what, nine or ten months ago? I told you how Mom cried when it came. You should call them. It would make them really happy."

"Don't be too sure about that. Hey, we left the beer on the porch. I don't know about you, but I could sure use another one."

I'd rather start to unpack, but I follow my brother back down to the porch. Red and yellow petals are falling from the sky.

I look up. There's a guy on the second-story balcony dead-heading rosebushes. He's slight, with spiky blue hair.

"Were you sleeping up there again, you slacker?" Nick calls up to him.

The guy grins, pinches off some more dead blooms, and aims them at Nick's head.

"C'mon down! You need to meet my sister!"

The guy climbs up onto the porch railing, grabs a thick nearby branch, and swings out into the tree. He's barefoot. It doesn't take him long to get to the ground. He looks like some new blue-crested species of monkey.

"Hi! I'm Charles."

"I'm Battle. That was impressive."

"Just faster than going through the house. Nice to meet you!"

"Charles is a man of many talents," Nick says, smiling. "Cooking's another. Speaking of which, you should get going on dinner, dude—Battle's been on the road all day."

"If you help, it'll be ready that much sooner."

Nick shakes his head. "No, we're exhausted. We're going to take a moment for a beverage. But we'll *so* appreciate dinner when it's ready," he says, sounding like he means it. He flashes Charles a smile, and Charles shakes his head, but then goes into the house.

Drinking more will confirm Robert's rapidly formed opinion of me, but I'm hot and tired and thirsty, and the beer's still cold.

Nick and I sit next to each other on the porch swing. Nearby there's a coffee can full of cigarette butts and sand. I wonder how often someone kicks it over.

Then I really look at Nick, trying to see how he's changed.

He won't talk to Mom and Dad; he's been clear on that since he first found me online. It was only after I harassed him for weeks that he finally sent them that one postcard from New York, right before he moved to Portland. Dad almost ripped it up, but Mom stopped him. I think it's still on the refrigerator.

When Nick and I IM, mostly he tells me funny stories about the people who ride in his cab. He's never said why he ran away, what happened between the time he left North Carolina and when he got to New York, how (and why) he went from New York to Portland, how he acquired a cab driver's license.

But then, I haven't asked.

Charles sticks his blue head out the front door. "Dinner in about five, you two."

"You are the true and living God," Nick says, and we follow Charles into the kitchen.

Robert and Aurora are at opposite ends of the long rectangular wooden table. It has benches on either side, instead of chairs, and looks like it was maybe designed as outdoor furniture. Nick sits across from Meryl. Charles fills a bowl for me, and I sit between Meryl and Aurora.

"So, what brings you to Portland?" Robert asks, looking at my beer, not me. He sounds like he wants to ask, "What would it take to make you leave?"

"I'll be starting at Reed this fall," I say.

"Figures," Robert says.

"Fuckin' Reedies," Charles says, but he's smiling, and I choose to interpret the comment as friendly.

Charles's dinner is fantastic: stir-fried spicy tofu, broccoli lightly steamed with a little garlic and lemon, served over the best brown rice I've ever had. It's like an antidote to the beer, and I feel more human, less like I'm going to collapse.

"Reed is an *excellent* school," Aurora says, glaring at Robert.

"She's a supergenius," Nick says. "She's gonna save all the little baby animals."

I used to think I wanted to be a vet. Then one of my dogs got hurt. I asked if I could watch the vet while he worked. He said yes.

I threw up.

"Shut up." I reach across the table to punch Nick on the arm.

Meryl says, "Now, kids, play nice."

Nick says, "No way. We've got a lot of sibling rivalry to catch up on." He grins at me.

Is that why I'm here?

When everyone's finished eating, I offer to do the dishes because it seems like the right thing to do. Aurora and Robert argue their way upstairs, and Meryl just leaves the house, without telling anyone where she's going.

Nick and Charles stay in the kitchen while I work. After a few minutes, Charles gets up from the table and starts drying.

"Hey, you shouldn't be doing that," Nick says to Charles. "You cooked!"

"Well, I didn't see you about to pick up the dishrag—be my guest," Charles says, tossing the wet rag at my brother. Nick tosses it back.

"No, no, you two have a good rhythm going. It's a pleasure to watch you work."

Nick stretches out on one of the benches and smiles. He's not that tall, and he's certainly not fat, but somehow, he still takes up a lot of space in the room.

Charles and I finish the dishes.

"So, I've got to work, but I can drop you guys off at the grocery first," Nick says.

I'd rather get back up to my room, unpack a little, and crash. But the way Nick says it makes me think that buying groceries is something that's required of me as a new member of the household, so I don't protest.

Charles and I climb into Nick's cab, and I have to plug my nose. "God, Nick," I say, "it smells like something died back here—what the hell?"

"You don't want to know. Just roll down the windows; it won't be much longer."

"Ask him about his worst fare," Charles says.

"What, you mean *you*?" Nick asks.

I already know the story of his worst fare—some guy who drunkenly expounded about his political philosophy for forty-five minutes while Nick drove him into the hinterlands. Then he relieved himself on the seat, and proved not to have a wallet. That was one of the first stories Nick told me when he tracked me down—after he'd verified his identity by telling me my middle name (Hall—after the building where our parents met), the color of the carpet in our living room (a trick question: a Persian rug), and Dad's favorite part of the Bible (the Song of Songs, always embarrassing).

It disturbed me how quickly I got used to being in touch again, and how much I'd worry when days would go by and I didn't hear from him.

I squint at Nick's cab-driver ID. His hair's shorter, his earrings aren't in, and he's wearing a button-down. "You look old in that picture."

"That's 'cause I *am* old."

"How late are you working tonight?" Charles asks.

"As long as they need me."

"Mister Overtime over here."

"Hey, once the show starts, I won't be able to take many shifts. I need to get in a lot of hours before then."

"The show Aurora and Meryl were talking about before?" I ask.

"You didn't tell her?" Charles asks.

Nick stops in front of a Safeway. "Here you go. See y'all later. Battle, don't believe a word he says."

I watch my brother pull back out into traffic.

"So, what should I not believe you about?"

Charles puts an arm around me and smiles. "Never mind. Let's buy groceries. You push the cart and I'll fill it."

"Okay."

"We used to rotate the grocery shopping, but after a few too many nights of ramen, box mac and cheese, and frozen pizza, I took it upon myself."

Charles removes a peach from the sweet-smelling pyramid near the front of the store and squeezes it gently, then nods and puts it into the cart.

"So, how does that work?" I ask. "You don't just pay for all the food?"

"Oh, God, no. Everyone chips in. Well, that's the theory, anyway."

I take out my wallet. "How much do you need for today?"

"Twenty?"

"Okay. What else am I responsible for?"

Charles scoops baby spinach into a plastic bag. "I take it you haven't gotten the rundown about how Forest House operates?"

Nick said it was kind of like a co-op, so I looked up co-ops online, but I kept finding contradictory information, and I lost four hours reading a year's worth of house meeting minutes from someplace in the Midwest. They wanted to kick this one guy out for never doing chores or showing up to meetings. But since he never showed up to meetings, it took them most of the year.

"I know how much rent is, but I don't know, like, who I pay or anything."

Charles twirls the bag of spinach and then ties a knot at the top.

"You are extremely lucky," he says. "You pay Aurora instead of an evil property-management company. And you didn't hear it from me, but she's been known to forget about charging. She owns Forest House outright, so the rent is gravy. Your brother collects for utilities. Oh, and breakfast and lunch are usually individual, but we all switch off cooking dinner."

"What do Robert and Meryl do?"

"In the house, or to pay the rent?"

"Both, I guess."

"Meryl teaches swimming at a community center. She cleans the bathrooms. Robert's a system administrator. He sweeps and mops. And you, by the way, will be dealing with recycling."

"Okay. Um, what about you?"

"Well, let's see. To pay the bills, I'm the world's oldest bike messenger, as long as my knees hold out. In the house, it's grocery shopping and gardening."

World's oldest? He's not old.

"For the house . . . are there, like, meetings?"

Charles laughs. "Not really, no. Between Forest House and the theater, we all spend more than enough time together."

"Is that how you all met?"

"Yep."

I'm trying not to be upset that Charles is the one to share all this useful information with me, and that Nick didn't bother to get time off for my first day in town, but I tell myself that it's good that he has a job. I can just hear Dad making some snide comment about how it's about time Nick developed a work ethic.

Meanwhile we've been making our way around the Safeway, accumulating an assortment of healthier food than I would have thought a group of people my age would voluntarily purchase. Then again, I guess none of them *are* my age.

"How old are you?" I ask Charles.

"Don't worry, I've got ID," he assures me. Among the healthy food items are a few bottles of cheap red wine.

"That's not why, I just wanted to know."

"How old do you think I am?" he asks.

The blue hair and the lip ring make it harder to tell.

"Twenty?"

"Twenty-seven."

Nine years older than me. Six years older than Nick.

How old is Meryl?

I try not to look nervous when the cashier rings up the wine. Charles gets carded, but she doesn't ask me to show mine. Maybe the bags under my eyes help.

"How do we get this back to the house?"

"We'll take the bus—it gets us within a few blocks."

Why didn't I just drive?

Oh, right. I wanted to see my brother.

The bus smells better than Nick's cab. Charles and I and our groceries sit near the back. It's not very crowded. I see five people reading. They all have chunky, black-framed glasses. Everyone on the bus looks a little dishevelled, like they all woke up late after sleeping in their clothes and had to leave the house without showering. On several people, this is a surprisingly good look.

"So, did you grow up in Portland?" I ask Charles.

He shakes his head. "I've lived a lot of places," he says vaguely.

I nod. I can't think of anything to say after that, and it seems like he can't, either, or maybe he just doesn't want to talk. Which is fine—I don't always want to talk, either. But a few times, I catch him looking hard at me. It's not like he's checking me out, more like he's trying to *figure* me out. Each time I see him doing it, he looks away.

I'm crashing. I've just closed my eyes when Charles says, "This is our stop." I make myself get up, sleepwalk the four blocks back to Forest House, and help him put the groceries away. Then I stagger up the stairs to my new room.

But before I can go to sleep, I have to inflate my air mattress and find the box with sheets and pillowcases in it. I bought the air mattress because I knew I was only going to be here for a couple of months before orientation, and there'll be a bed in my dorm room. Besides the air mattress, my "furniture" is two folding bookcases, two cardboard dressers, and a folding laundry hamper. Not classy, but it all fit in my car. And I kind of love how temporary it is.

I miss my dogs, Dante and Beatrice. But I always miss them in the summers.

I've spent the past three summers away from my dogs—and Mom and Dad. On the surface, that seems like the opposite of what would happen. One of your children runs away, so you send the other one to camp for three months?

I don't know. Maybe they thought I should expand my horizons. The first year it was a ballet camp, which I loathed, and then the next two years, it was the Siegel Summer Institute for Gifted and Talented Youth.

Which expanded my horizons a lot more than Mom and Dad had bargained for.